SnowFall

Sierra Conrady

DEDICATION

I want to thank my sister Brittany and my Sister in law for always pushing me to finish this book, without their guidance and constant advice Gracelia wouldn't be who she is today. I also want to thank my mom for raising me and being the inspiration behind Hugh, he wouldn't be who is is today without her and Gracelia wouldn't have her dream without my mom raising me to always defy the social norms of today's society.

CONTENTS

PROLOGUE

The moonlight turned night into day as servants bustled around the mansion. The light from the windows casting their shadows onto the ground as they ran. The breeze going through the trees suddenly became violent as if a tornado was coming through the valley. The shutters rattled on their hinges as the wind whipped against them like a banshee's howl. Inside the mansion in the master room a woman screamed from pain, doctors huddled together around her. She was breathing hard from trying to bring a life into the world. Soon she collapsed, but the baby did not cry, the doctors looked at each other worried. However, the woman's husband rushed through the door with concern.

"Is the baby all right?" The doctors turned and bowed their heads, one maid carried the baby over to the man.

"We aren't sure my lord."

"Give the baby here." The maid handed the little bundle over to the man and as soon as she did the baby moved. Everyone in the room gasped in surprise, the man smiled.

"Dear," The woman on the bed told her husband. "Bring the baby over." The man walked over to his wife and sat beside her on the bed. As he handed the baby to her, she smiled. "She has white hair and rosy cheeks." The woman gently touched the baby's hand, to her surprise her daughter grabbed her finger tightly with a smile. "I think I have the perfect name for our daughter Hugh." She looked up at her husband, he was smiling at his two girls with love in his eyes. He put his hand on her head, smoothing the hairs that were standing up.

"What do you have in mind my dear Juliana?" Hugh asked. Juliana looked down at the small baby in her arms, milk white skin, rosy cheeks and white hair reflected the color of the moon's rays outside her window. The staff gasped as they looked outside, the snow was falling from the clouds but the sky was still lit up by the moon.

"It's the first snow!" A maid told one of the doctors.

"The Goddess of winter blesses this child. They say when a child is born, and it snows, it will bless them and have a good life." A maid said while looking at Juliana. Juliana looked up at the maid and back to her daughter.

"Hugh, due to it being the first snow. I think we should name her Gracelia." Juliana said with a smile that reached her eyes. Her curly brown hair falling around her small face, her brown eyes filling with tears as she looked at the small child in her arms who she had carried for nine long months. Hugh put his arm around her shoulders and kissed the top of her head.

"I think it's a beautiful name my love. Fits our beautiful daughter perfectly." Juliana and Hugh looked out the window with the staff as the snow began falling past while Gracelia slept in her mother's arms. The wind howled softly outside as if not to wake the sleeping child.

CHAPTER ONE

Sunlight shined through the window, hitting the young girls closed eyes. She tossed and turned in her bed, grabbing the doll her father had given her for her second birthday. She opened her eyes once she knew she couldn't go back to sleep. Sitting up, her curly white hair fell around her shoulders like a curtain of satin. She lifted her tiny fist to rub her eyes; she opened them and looked out the window. Her sapphire blue eyes reflecting the light making them seem as if they were glowing. She turned when she heard her door open, "Young Mistress! You're already awake?" The voice came from her nanny, Adelina, her brown hair pulled into a braid like bun on the top of her head.

"Yes, I'm awake already because someone left the curtains open." She said to Adelina, wondering why her nanny suddenly looked so flustered.

"I closed them last night! I was sure of it!" Adelina said with a huff, trying to pick her brain to remember last night before she left the little girl's room.

"It's all right Adelina. It's fine it was open, because I get to go wake up mama and papa!" The little girl said with a smile that reached her eyes.

"Well young Gracelia, your father is already awake and working in his office seeing as he didn't sleep with the Duchess but fell asleep on the couch there instead last night." Gracelia crossed her arms over her chest and huffed.

7

"No fair! It's MY birthday! I wanted to wake them up!" Adelina laughed at how cute the young mistress was and walked over to her bed to sit beside her.

"Well, the Duchess is still asleep if you wish to go wake her up." Adelina winked at Gracelia and patted her head. Hearing that Gracelia instantly brightened like a lotus flower blooming in spring.

"I wanna go wake up mama Ade!" Gracelia held out her arms to Adelina with a smile. "Carry me?" Adelina got up from the bed and picked up the young mistress cradling Gracelia in her arms, forgetting how light she was for a six-year-old.

"Shall we, my lady?" Adelina asked her young mistress.

"Lets!" Gracelia said with a smile and pointed towards the door. "Let's go!" Adelina carried the young girl out of the room and down the hall, they passed maids who bowed to Gracelia, she waved while smiling at everyone. "Good morning!" She said to every maid they passed. Gracelia differed from most noble children, she cared about the people that worked under her father and mother. She wasn't a spoiled kid because her mother came from a family that had fallen out of the emperors' graces when they didn't send her eldest sister to become his concubine. However when Gracelia's father had met her mother, he fell in love with her at first sight and his family, the De Mornica's, were the right hands of the Emperor. They controlled one of the kingdom's largest armies, according to her father that is.

They came to a stop in front of a big oak door with two knights standing guard. They bowed to Gracelia as Adelina put her down. "She's come to wake the Duchess." Adelina told the knights in a hushed tone. The knights looked at each other trying to hold a giggle in as to not wake the Duchess before Gracelia could. They opened the door just enough for the tiny mistress to slip through. Gracelia slowly made her way over to her mother's bed, trying to step as lightly as possible on the old wood floors. Soon she came to a stop on her father's side of the bed and slowly climbed up, she lifted herself up onto the bed and crawled slowly over to her mother. When she was sure she was asleep and not faking it she jumped into action. Jumping on her mom she yelled, " Time to wake up! Daddy's little princess said so!"

"Ugh... What time is it?" Her mother asked, slightly annoyed but happy at the same time.

"I don't know mommy but GET UP! It's my birthday!" Gracelia said, poking Juliana's cheek. She sat up and looked at the young white-haired blue eyed child in her lap.

"You know, I think you've gained weight my darling." Her mother said trying to suppress her laughter at her daughter's face of shock.

"MAMA! Have I really?" Gracelia asked while checking her arms, wrists, legs, tummy and cheeks. When she suddenly noticed her mom smiling, she poked her mom's chest and crossed her arms. "Not funny!"

"It's a little funny to see my child's little face get so shocked at what her mother tells her." The Duchess laughed as she pulled Gracelia to her chest. "You're just too cute my little one." Gracelia wrapped her arms around the Duchess' neck and sat her head on her chest. She could hear her mother's soft heartbeat under her ear. Since she was used to the sound, Juliana once told her it was because she carried her in her belly for nine months and that's all she heard.

"Mommy!" Gracelia yelled as she picked up her head. "I'm Seven today!" The Duchess laughed.

"You were born when the moon was at its highest peak while the first snow fell. So, I'm sure you aren't seven till then." She poked Gracelia's nose with a smile, she huffed at her mother.

"NO! I'm seven!" The Duchess laughed at her child's puffed up face as if she was fooling anyone to make them think she was mad.

"Where's Adelina?" Gracelia's face brightened at the mention of her nanny's name.

"She's waiting outside mommy." She pointed her tiny finger towards the door.

"Adelina! Please come in!" The door opened and Adelina walked over to the bed and bowed to the Duchess.

"Good morning, Duchess Juliana. What can I do for you today?" Adelina asked, in a soft voice she only uses with nobles.

"Could you please have one of the knights

outside tell my husband to join us for breakfast this morning and please take Gracelia back to her room to get dressed. Also, since she is seven, she can walk on her own now." Adelina bowed again.

"Yes, my lady. Right away." Adelina turned and went over to the half-open door and poked her head out to tell the knight to deliver the Duchess' words to the Duke. Adelina came back to the bed and looked at Gracelia. "Now young mistress shall we go so your mother may get dressed, hmm? Would you like to wear that blue dress that your father ordered for you from the tailor yesterday?" Gracelia looked at her mother and was about to open her mouth to say something when Juliana spoke.

"Go get dressed so we can eat yummy food hmm?" Juliana said as she kissed her daughter's forehead. Gracelia smiled and nodded, she got off the bed and followed Adelina out as maids came in to tend to the Duchess, get her dressed and ready for the day. Gracelia watched as the door shut behind them.

"Tell the chief to prepare breakfast for the morning and make sure he doesn't put too much sugar in the young mistress' tea or she'll be bouncing off the walls after." Adelina said to a maid that was walking past, the maid turned and was about to leave but saw Gracelia and bowed. Gracelia smiled at the maid as she disappeared down the hall. She held Adelina's hand as they walked down the hall, when they passed an open window. Gracelia stopped, pulling her hand away from Adelina, she walked over to the window and looked out. There was smoke billowing out from the baker's shop as people's day began. The sun was high in the sky and a breeze was rustling the trees foretelling of the coming winter as it had a bite to it. The clouds passed by as though they're saying good morning to all the townspeople. In the mansion's square, she saw the knights of the first squadron shooting arrows at targets and sparring with one another.

Gracelia always dreamed of being a knight but she knew that was unbecoming to a lady. She had decided that for her seventh birthday she would ask her father to teach her swordsmanship and archery. The breeze stopped for a minute and she could hear the bubbling of the brook outside the mansion's walls, the voices of the townspeople below in the valley haggling their wares and the laughter of the young woman sitting in the shade on the street. "Are you alright mistress?" Adelina asked Gracelia, following her gaze to the knights. "Is there a knight you suddenly fancy?" Gracelia coughed at the thought.

"Nope! I wanna be like them one day!" Adelina gasped with surprise but quickly knelt down to look at Gracelia.

"You can be whatever you want to be Gracelia. A lady should know how to protect herself, should the need arise," Gracelia looked at Adelina with admiration. She had told no one about her dream because she was afraid to be yelled at. So hearing

those words from Adelina filled her with hope.
"Let's keep walking and I'll tell you a story from my
childhood." Gracelia grabbed Adelina's hand and
kept walking. "When I was a young girl, living in
the town below us, my father owned the blacksmith
forge which my brother now runs. My father was a
jolly man but he thought that girls can't always be
protected by their fathers or brothers. So one day he
forged me a small iron dagger to keep on my waist,
in case of danger. He told me how to wield it and
where to strike at a person if they tried to harm me.
What I'm trying to say is, don't let anyone tell you,
you can't be something just because you're a girl
young mistress. You never know, maybe you'll be
better than those knights down there."

Gracelia looked at the tapestries on the wall as
they passed, telling stories from the De Mornica
line and how there weren't any female knights on
them. She thought maybe one day she'll be on one
of those tapestries in shining armor surrounded by
knights that followed her and how she'd be the one
to protect those she loves.

CHAPTER TWO

Gracelia sat in front of the mirror as the maids braided her hair into two parts and added blue flower pins to match the blue dress she was wearing. The bow on the collar was a deep gray satin, the white ruffles on the hem of the skirt made the dress stop above her ankles, the sleeves were light blue lace that showed off her slender arms the maids had compared to those of her mother, Duchess Juliana. Since she was too young, they didn't dare put makeup on her milk white skin and her cheeks were already rosy enough. Once the maids were happy they stepped away from the young girl. Gracelia gasped at her reflection in the mirror, she looked stunning almost like a young lady. "Are we done?" She asked the maids, they smiled in response and bowed to her.

"Can you do a spin for us my lady?" Asked Adelina. Gracelia spun in a circle and felt the skirt lift making a closed blossom around her legs. She smiled and giggled, the maids all gasped at the stunning young girl in front of the mirror. They couldn't believe how much she'd grown in the past year.

"I feel pretty Ade!" Gracelia said, still smiling wide. Adelina walked over to her and knelt down, fixing one pin that had moved from the spin.

"You're always pretty young mistress," She smiled at her. "Even with bed head." Gracelia poked Adelina on the nose and stuck out her tongue.

"Should we get going? Your mother and father must be waiting for you." Adelina offered the young girl her hand and together they left the room. Gracelia suddenly felt nervous, and she bit her lip, she would do it. She would ask her father for lessons on swordsmanship and archery, she wanted to be just like her papa. However, her little heart beat faster, and she suddenly felt nauseous. Adelina looked down at Gracelia and stopped, kneeling in front of her, "Are you alright young mistress? You don't look well. Is the dress too small or is your hair too tight?" Gracelia shook her head which only made her more nauseous. "Then what's wrong?" Gracelia squeezed Adelina's hand.

"I'm nervous." Adelina looked at her worried. "I'm gonna ask papa for my birthday present."

"That's a good thing, there's no way he could tell you no. You're his little girl."

~~~~~~~~~~

"No." Said Gracelia's father to her birthday present she wanted. Her mother just looked at her daughter, dumbfounded at what she had just asked Hugh.

"But papa! I wanna learn how to use a sword! Plus, I wanna learn archery too!" Gracelia begged to her papa, he sat there looking at her, not touching his food, the fork laid on the plate half dug into his roasted chicken breast.

"I said no." Hugh said, picking up his fork again. "That's unbecoming of a noble lady Gracelia! You can't be serious? Do you know what the others

15

would say?" Duchess Juliana asked her, Gracelia pleaded with her mother.

"Mama! Daddy's a Duke! They wouldn't dare say anything! Plus, I could train in secret, no one would know!" The Duchess shook her head and her father just stared at her, the fork halfway to his mouth. "Plus, it's my birthday, and that's what I want. I want daddy to teach me!"

"Gracelia, I don't know about this. You're a girl and a young girl at that. You're only seven!" Her mother told her, her brown eyes pleading with her to drop the subject. However, Gracelia was a noble by birth and still had pride in what she believed in.

"I don't care! Boys learn how to fight and wield swords when they turn seven! Why can't I?" Gracelia would stand her ground on what she wanted, she never asked or begged for anything and this time this is what she wanted with all her heart. Her father lowered his fork and motioned for a knight to come to him. Gracelia noticed it was Sir Lee, her father's second in command to the first squadron. Sir Lee nodded, making his black hair move slightly out of place, his dark brown eyes came to rest on Gracelia.

"Your grace, I sincerely think it is not a good idea. From a knight's point, I would highly recommend you drop the topic. Learning how to use a sword isn't child's play. It is a dangerous weapon, and it takes more lives than saves them." Gracelia lowered her head and clenched her fists into her dress and shouted.

"I DON'T CARE! THIS IS WHAT I WANT! I KNOW THE DANGERS!!" Suddenly the whole room was quiet as if everyone was holding their breath to see what would happen next. Before Gracelia knew it, she ran out of the dinning room and slammed the door behind her, leaving her mother and father staring after her in disbelief.

~~~~~~~~

Juliana looked at her husband in confusion. "What's gotten into her suddenly?" Juliana looked at the empty seat where her daughter was sitting just a minute prior. Hugh shook his head, his brown hair shifting, he looked up at his wife with sapphire blue eyes.

"I'm not sure. Maybe we've been too lenient with her. We give her everything she could ever hope for. I thought we raised her better than this," He said pointing towards the closed door. "She's acting like a spoiled child. Maybe it's time she sees what it's like in the real world. Outside of our borders." Juliana gasped.

"You can't be serious? She's a child Hugh! She's only seven, showing her what it's like will scar her. She'll be afraid to even leave the house," Juliana shivered in her seat despite the warm sun resting on her back. "I won't allow it. Any of it!" Before Hugh could answer, a knight called into the room.

"My lord! Sir Marcus has just arrived!" Hugh sighed and put down his fork. Standing up he walked over to his wife and kissed her forehead, pushing a pin back into place to hold her large curls.

17

"Seems we must cut breakfast short my love. We'll figure something else out I suppose." He looked over at Sir Lee as he made his way to the door. "Go find my daughter and lock her up in her room, under no circumstances is she allowed to leave it. Make sure her nanny and maids know as well or whip them should they let her out of the room." Lee bowed to Hugh as he left the room and Lee followed, leaving Juliana to sit alone staring at her plate and half-empty cup of tea.

~~~~~~~~~

Gracelia ran until she couldn't run anymore, she bent over, wheezing. Tears clouded her vision, she wiped angrily at her face, causing a blue flower pin to fall to the ground and rest on the carpet. The young girl looked up and saw she was in the library, a place she associated with safety and comfort. She closed the door behind her and walked along the shelves, sliding her finger across the spines. She breathed in the smell of old books and leather. Then she suddenly heard a gasp and a book fall to the ground. She looked up quickly to see a boy not much older than her standing next to the library window. He had silver hair and green eyes like a forest during twilight. Gracelia collected herself and raised her head the way she has seen her mother do when being greeted by guests from lower houses.

"Who are you and what are you doing in my library?" She asked the boy, he didn't move but didn't seem scared.

"Who are you if I may ask?" The boy answered

18

back. Gracelia pursed her lips and stood up straighter.

"I asked you first, the rule is men are to introduce themselves to ladies first if they enter their home." Gracelia said, challenging the boy. He shook his head in defeat and bowed.

"I am Nicholas Rune, son to Marcus Rune the chancellor to his royal highness the Emperor. Who are you?" Gracelia knew what to do and instantly curtsied to the boy, her white braids falling around her shoulders.

"I am Gracelia Da Mornica, the daughter of Duke Hugh Da Mornica." The boy snorted at her.

"The rumors said you are gorgeous and pretty but I don't see it in the slightest." Gracelia's jaw dropped at that comment, she wanted badly to snap at the boy but she knew her father would have her head if she disgraced the Emperors' chancellors' son. If she did anything too rash, the boy would definitely run to his father and complain. Before she could answer, Sir Lee opened the door, took a peek inside and saw the young mistress with the young boy. He walked over to Gracelia without a word and stood in front of her, his hand on the hilt of his sword. He looked at the boy up and down and saw a dagger on the boy's hip.

"Who are you?" Before Nicholas could answer Gracelia cut him off.

"Sir Lee, I'm tired. I want to go lay down." She said, putting her hand on the knight's arm. Sir Lee turned and pushed her out of the room.

"Yes, my lady. We have much to discuss as well per your father's order." Before the door shut behind them, Gracelia stuck her tongue out at Nicholas and waved. When the door shut Nicholas in the library, he just stood there dumbfounded at what had just happened.

The young boy scoffed, picked up the book he had dropped and looked out the window at the knights below. The sunlight hit the spine of the book and written in gold the title read 'The Da Mornica Lineage'.

CHAPTER THREE

"I believe what you're trying to say is that you won't consider the Emperor's offer?" A man with silver hair said, shaking his head. He looked at Hugh with intense hazel eyes. "It's a rather good offer Hugh." Hugh shook his head in defiance and rubbed his temples as his childhood friend stood in front of his desk. "Just think about it Hugh. She's the perfect candidate to be the Empress to the crowned Prince. The temple of Winter said the Goddess will bless the marriage herself. What more could you ask for? She already stands out with her hair and the eyes she has, which are much brighter than yours."

"Marcus, I don't know why you're even trying. She's too young to even be considered, she's only seven." He told Marcus, trying to defend his daughter, but Marcus wasn't having it.

"Come on Hugh. I tried to offer him my daughter, but he rejected it, specifically said your daughters name." Marcus told Hugh, leaning on the front of the desk on his hands. "The crowned Prince is ten, what more could you ask for? They're only three years apart in age. Unlike you and your wife." Hugh looked up at Marcus with eyes that could murder. " You're what? Thirty-eight now? And she's thirty if I remember correctly. You had Gracelia when you were thirty-one and your wife was twenty-three, maybe twenty-four. I don't pay attention to age, much too busy helping the

Emperor and all."

"Marcus I said no, and that's the end, I have enough on my mind as it is." Marcus seemed to perk up at those words.

"Tell me old friend, what's got you in a mood? Hmm? Maybe your precious daughter isn't so precious anymore?" Hugh slammed his hand on the desk, in his mind he could see Gracelia in a red dress next to the crowned prince and it disgusted him.

"Leave her out of this! I am her father!" Hugh told him, angry. "I do not wish to talk about it with you when you came here to propose my daughter be engaged to the crown prince." Marcus shook his head in disbelief.

"My lord! Duchess Juliana is here to see you!" Hugh sighed and Marcus looked over at the door.

'Great. Another thing to add fuel to the fire.' Hugh thought to himself. He looked at Marcus. "No word of what you said to my wife!" Marcus put his hands up in defeat. "Enter." After he said that, Juliana entered with a flustered expression on her face. Hugh quickly stood up and put his hands on her shoulders. "Are you alright?" He asked her with worry in his voice. She waved her hand at him.

"I'm fine. I've just been thinking is all, and I came here to talk to you about it." She looked over and saw Marcus. Pulling away from Hugh, Juliana curtsied to Marcus. "Good Morning Chancellor Marcus." Marcus bowed to her and looked over at Hugh.

"Just think about it, I won't be so nice next time.
I'll try to keep it a secret." Hugh glared at him as
Marcus left the room. Julianna looked from the door
to Hugh.

"What was that about?"

"Nothing to concern yourself about dear. Just
some problems with one report I sent in, I fixed it.
Now what is it you need to see me about?" Hugh
said, sitting on the couch, he motioned his wife to
sit next to him, Juliana walked over and sat down.

"I've been thinking about what Gracelia said she
wanted." Hugh scoffed.

"You can't be serious Juliana." He put his head
on his hand and looked at his wife in disbelief.

"I was thinking, what if we let her try to learn?
Maybe it's just a phase, she'll see it's too hard for
her delicate body and quit and go back to being our
little girl." Juliana said, trying to find any loopholes
she could grab onto.

"What if that doesn't work Juliana?" Hugh asked
her.

"Then you train her like she's a man, she'll see
she can't even compare to the other knights." Hugh
looked at her and smiled.

"I think that might work but what if she hates
me for it?" Hugh said, suddenly not smiling
anymore and genuinely worried about his only child
hating him. Julianna put her hand on his knee.

"She'll get over it, she's a child. She'll see later
down the road that what you did was the best for
her. You showed her she can't live up to a man's

status." Hugh laughed at that remark, Juliana looked at him in confusion.

"I remember when you said the same thing to your younger sister about becoming a high-ranking official. How she wouldn't be able to because that's a man's status." Juliana smacked his knee.

"Well now look at her, she's married to a Duke as well and has two children with a third one on the way." She told him, trying to find any reasoning that her daughter wouldn't quit after a day of training.

"Fine, I guess we'll try it I suppose. But if she doesn't quit after the first day then you will have to take care of the matter as her mother and head of the house." Hugh told her, putting a hand on her cheek. Juliana nodded her head in understanding.

"I know, when the time comes, I'll figure it out." Juliana leaned in and kissed her husband. She had to make Gracelia see she would never become a knight.

~~~~~~~~~

Gracelia sat on her bed staring out the window, arms over her chest with her back to the door. Adelina stood next to the door, after being told what had happened with the young mistress, she didn't know what to do or say. All the other maids were too afraid to stay in the room with Gracelia because she was a wild child that didn't listen to rules. Adelina watched the young girls back as she saw her slowly break down. Adelina knew Gracelia desperately wanted to be like her father, a hero of war. However, the silence was deafening to Adelina,

before she could say anything Gracelia broke the
silence.

"What's so wrong about wanting to be different?
It's not fair." Adelina sighed, went over to the young
mistress and sat beside her on the bed.

"I know my lady. Maybe you could try again?
Maybe I could try to reason with your father too,
perhaps? My family made his sword he carries
around, that's why he offered me the job to be your
nanny." Adelina put her arm around the young girl.

"I doubt it'll work Ade. Father's just too
stubborn to see things my way. He sees it like he's
still at war and I hate it! I don't want to be a fragile
girl who runs and hides at the sight of a fight. I want
to help, I don't want to be useless." After Gracelia
said that, she cried. Adelina pulled her closer, letting
Gracelia cry into her lap. Rubbing Gracelia's hair
always seemed to calm her down when she was a
small child. When she suddenly heard the door
open, Adelina quickly stood up. Gracelia rubbed her
eyes and stared out the window at the sun, trying to
dry her tears. Hugh came in through the door and
rubbed the back of his head. Adelina quickly
bowed.

"Hello my lord. What may I help you with?"
Adelina asked him, curious as to why he was in his
daughter's room.

"I need to speak with Gracelia in private."
Adelina looked over at the young mistress and
headed for the door, she passed by Hugh and slowly
shut the door.

"Gracelia." Hugh started.

"What?" She said back.

"We need to talk, may I come sit next to you?" He asked his daughter, he wasn't used to her being angry at him like this. Gracelia didn't answer, so he sat at the edge of her bed, away from her.

"What is it father?" Hugh flinched, she only called him father if she was angry at him.

"About what you wanted for your birthday. Your mother and I were talking and well," Hugh rubbed his temples. "We will let you try but if it gets too hard you have to quit, understand?" Gracelia quickly stood up and ran to her father. She threw her arms around him with a smile.

"Thank you papa! Thank you! I won't let you down! I'll try really hard to be as great as you!" Gracelia climbed onto her father's lap and sat there hugging him, Hugh slowly put his arms around his daughter, hoping his wife was right. Adelina opened the door just a crack and saw Gracelia sitting on the Duke's lap and smiled.

'I hope they worked everything out.' She thought to herself, she slowly shut the door. Not knowing what the Duke and Duchess had up their sleeves to try and make Gracelia quit on the first day of training.

CHAPTER FOUR

Gracelia opened her eyes as soon as the sunlight hits her face, she was excited and ready to start her training. Today was the day she'd prove to her father she could do it, be a knight like him. She threw off her blankets and jumped out of bed, her white curly mesh on top of her head. She had slept fitfully last night because of her excitement for today. She ran over to her door and opened it. To her surprise, a knight was standing outside her door. "Excuse me?" She said in a soft voice to the knight, the man turned his head, his eyes opened in shock.

"Young mistress! You're already awake?" Gracelia nodded her head.

"Who are you?"

"My name is Marquis," He bowed to her. "A pleasure to meet you my lady." Gracelia felt her blood rising to her cheeks, making her skin a light shade of mother rose pink. Upon further inspection, she saw that he had black hair and even darker eyes, his eyes reminded her of the black opal's she had seen on her father's ceremonial rapier. Gracelia lowered her eyes to the ground.

"Thank you, a pleasure to meet you as well, Marquis." As Gracelia closed the door, Marquis bowed to her. She put her back up against the door once it was closed and she heard the familiar click. It surprised her to see another knight, she had only ever met Sir Lee. She couldn't help but notice he was handsome, she shook her head at the thought.

"I'm only seven!" She told herself under her breath, walking over to the windows that looked out into the courtyard she saw that the sun was finally rising over the trees. She opened her balcony door and walked out into the sunlight. She shivered in her sleeping gown despite the sun's warm rays. She loved looking at the world on her balcony, it was one thing she admired the most about her parents, it seemed to her like they knew this room was for her. The breeze blew a lock of her white hair into her face and she grabbed it. Twirling it in her hand, she sighed. Gracelia knew she had grown up and didn't act her age and many commented on it, even her nanny once told her that while she was reading a five hundred page book in the library when she was five.

Many also commented on the fact her hair didn't match either of her parents as they both had brown hair. Gracelia didn't understand why but Adelina had told her one night while she stayed up crying, feeling like an animal in a cage whenever new guests would come to see her family, that she was born on the night of the first snow. The wet-nurse had told her parents, Goddess of Winter had blessed her and would lead a life full of love and prosperity.

"Love..." The word seemed foreign on her lips, she couldn't grasp the concept. She knew her father and mother loved each other and her very much but she didn't see the importance. She couldn't understand why love would lead people to war and anger so much like in the stories she had read.

Adelina had asked her to read a book she loved called Love Under The Moon but after the first chapter Gracelia had gotten bored with it. The books she loved the most told of knights in armor saving a far away kingdom or about knights fighting dragons.

To her, marriage and kids was a foreign concept. She knew better things were waiting for her than a simple life; she wanted a life of adventure and excitement. Tucking a strand of hair behind her ear, she watched as the sun rose higher and higher, welcoming her personally.

~~~~~~~~~

Gracelia paced in front of the windows to her balcony, the sunlight casting her small shadow onto the blue carpet beneath her feet. Adelina was late, later than usual, when suddenly the door opened to reveal a disheveled Adelina. In her hands was a bright blue box, she carefully carried it to Gracelia's bed and placed it on the satin sheets. "Sorry for the wait my lady, the tailor took longer than expected to make this for you on your Father's wishes." Gracelia walked over to the box, examining it. Adelina huffed beside her, winded from running from the village all the way up the hill to the mansion. Adelina smiled nervously at Gracelia's hesitance to open the blue box. "Are you alright?" She asked her young mistress, worried she was having second thoughts.

"Y... Yes!" Gracelia told Adelina, shaking herself from her thoughts. She was worried about what would be inside, if her father had kept his promise or had gifted her a new dress to make up for breaking it. While her hands were shaking, she reached for the box and her fingers grazed the cardboard. With a jerk, the lid came off easily. Gracelia gasped, inside was a light powder blue tunic with black pants. "Always blue..." She mumbled, ever since she had been born that fateful night, her mother and father showered her with gifts different shades of blue. Gracelia loved blue but sometimes it was overwhelming.

She looked over at her wardrobe, still in a frightful mess from her rummage for any clothes she could wear for training. All different shades of blue and white dresses littered the surrounding floor. She reached inside to touch the fabric, it was softer than she imagined it to be. On the front of the shirt was the Da Mornica sigil, a unicorn's horn wrapped in ivy. She laid it out on her bed and took out the black pants, these however weren't as soft. Under her tiny fingers it felt almost like wool, however it was still fall but the days had become brisk over the night following her birthday. She laid them next to each other, when something caught her eye at the bottom of the box, a shiny little thing but she reached in and rolled it into her palm. It was a tiny pin with a snowflake engraved with beads hanging off of it. Gracelia looked over at her nanny confused what to do with this tiny treasure.

"OH! THAT!" Adelina quickly took it from the young girls hand and put it in a lock of her hair.

"That's how you wear it, also wear it with a bun or ponytail. It's a symbol of your Noble birth." She pulled the young mistress over to her vanity. "Look in the mirror." Much to Gracelia's surprise, in her sea of white hair, the pin was a stark contrast with her hair. The beads hanging down moved when she turned her head, the engraved snowflake twinkling when she moved. Gracelia moved her tiny hand to cover her mouth, she didn't wear something this tiny in her hair. The blue flower pins she wore were bigger than this tiny treasure. She felt if it dropped, it would surely shatter.

"I can't wear this." She looked at her nanny in the mirror, Adelina looked at the young girl in surprise wondering why she wouldn't wear such an intricate piece. However to Gracelia, it was a reminder that she was a girl, boys didn't like pretty things such as this. She quickly took it out of her hair and placed it on the surface in front of her, watching it twinkle in the sunlight.

CHAPTER FIVE

Gracelia sat on the cold wooden bench in the courtyard eyes cast to the ground, the other knights were all gawking at her in the unfamiliar clothes she was wearing. Adelina had helped her tame her curls, and pulled it into high ponytail, the insignia stitched with off white and green thread catching their attention. She felt uncomfortable sitting there twiddling her thumbs, the shirt hanging loosely around her small frame, the black pants bunching at the knee showing her black lace up boots and rabbit fur socks underneath. She huffed in frustration, it was her first day of training and all she could do was sit and wait for her father or Sir Lee to assist her. The sound of yelling caught her attention, she lifted her head and saw two men arguing. "You know I'm better then you in a fight! I've never been injured!" Said one of the men who looked to be in his late to mid thirties.

"Yeah right! You're old! I'm younger and faster! I was hit by an arrow when it deflected off a shield." The other fired back. "You're shield if I recall!" This man was indeed younger, he couldn't be more then in his late twenties judging from how he held himself. Gracelia sighed and quickly strode over to them, the other knights parted for her, as if she was dangerous. What she didn't know was that she did have a dangerous air about her though, it seemed to cling to the very air she breathed. The young girl quickly stood in-between the men and stomped her foot.

"ENOUGH!" Both men quickly looked down at her, it didn't register that the voice that was filled with anger came from her. They ignored her and continued arguing, Gracelia felt her blood rising to her face in anger, as if she was a volcano about to explode. "Did you not hear me or you both deaf?" She quickly kicked one in the shin and stomped on the others foot with more strength then she thought she had. Both men hollered and held onto their leg and foot, the twenty year old jumping around like a one legged rabbit while the other just hissed in pain. She grabbed the older man's ear and pulled his face to hers. "NEXT TIME PAY ATTENTION WHEN A LADY SPEAKS!" She screamed at him. The man's eyes grew wide as Gracelia's eyes appeared to darken to an unnatural shade of ocean blue. Behind them, they heard clapping. Everyone looked up in unison to see Hugh clapping with Sir Lee behind him, his face a stone mask. All the knights kneeled with their hands in fists over their hearts.

"My lord!" They all said in unison, much to Gracelia's surprise even the one legged rabbit had kneeled his face still contorted in pain.

"Let him go my dear." Hugh said, ignoring all the knights, still on their knees. He looked at Gracelia in amusement as she let go of the man's ear. Once released he rubbed his ear as he to kneeled to their Duke. "I'm quite amazed at how you handled that situation." Gracelia looked at her father, still fuming.

"What else was a supposed to do? Let them act like children over an idiotic matter?" All the knights gasped at her choice of words, the rumors had been true. She was much more grown up then they realized for only being seven years old. She shrugged and shook her head, her hair swinging widely behind her. "To think they are the first squadron, useless." She spate the word like it was poison on her tongue. Hugh just laughed at his daughter partly in surprise but also in pride.

"I was waiting to see how you'd handle the situation my little snowflake." Gracelia walked over to her father, weaving in between the knights as she went. "I thought you'd cry or run at the sight of fighting. You surprise me my daughter. You acted as if you were their lord and commander." Gracelia stood beside her father, hands on her hips staring at the two soldiers that had been bickering. "What would you do if you were their commander?" Hugh looked down at his daughter, wondering what she'd do if she was in his shoes. Testing her character was one of things he wanted to see the most, the life of a knight isn't an easy one but what he heard come from his daughter surprised him even more then how she had reacted to the situation.

"I'd make them run until the sun set from the entrance of the village and back here." Gracelia looked up at her father, she was angry at how the men had acted. They were bothers in arms but instead acted as if they were small children, like children her age. She wasn't use to showing this side of her, she didn't even know she had it till a few minutes ago. Hugh smiled and looked at the two knights.

"You heard her, run!" The two men looked at each other and quickly fell to the ground and pleaded.

"Forgive us! We didn't mean to anger you my lord!" The older man said.

"Please, it wasn't meant to anger anyone! Please forgive us my lord!" Hugh laughed and looked at the two mean groveling in the dirt.

"I don't think it should be me, your asking for forgiveness. I'm not the one you angered." At that the men turned to Gracelia, repeating what they had told her father. Gracelia didn't know how to react, but from the books she had read she went with what usually happens in the stories in this kind of situation.

"You," She pointed to the older man. "What's you name?"

"My name is Tomas young mistress." Gracelia looked at him further as he looked at her. His eyes were a bark brown and his hair the same color, she could see that he didn't have a streak of gray in his hair. She looked at the younger man.

"And you?" The younger man lifted his head, he had eyes the color of the dark clouds that foretold rain, his hair a jet black like charcoal when a fires gone out.

"My name is Alexzander young mistress."
She smiled, she now knew their names and could
put faces to names. She looked up at the sun and
saw it was only half towards the center of the sky.
She looked at her father.

"Papa?" He looked at the men and then to
her, nodding. "What do you think I should do since
they apologized?" Hugh stifled a laugh behind his
gloved hand, his other hand on the hilt of his sword.

"That's for you to decide my dear. If you
wish to forgive them then go ahead, if not then you
decide what their punishment is." He watched as his
daughter's face broke out in a smile he knew all to
well from Juliana.

'This isn't going to be good' he thought to
himself, the last time he got that smile from Juliana
he had to sleep in his office for a week.

"You two," She pointed to each of them.
"Since you have so much energy to fight, you can
teach me how to wield a sword." The color faded
from their faces, they both looked at each other in
horror. They knew that teaching her when she didn't
very much like them wasn't going to be an easy
feat. Hugh couldn't hold it anymore, he laughed
even louder.

~~~~~~~~

"You two are HORRIBLE at teaching!"
Gracelia said as she glared at the two men, they
flinched at her harsh words. "AND YOU'RE
KNIGHTS OF THE FIRST SQUADRON?

HOW!?" Hugh watched as his daughter screamed at the two men, there was no denying she had an air of authority about her. He chuckled at the stunned looks on their faces, both men looked over to him as if asking for help. He shook his head, he wasn't going to help them. Both men looked defeated as their shoulders slumped forward. "I take it back, you're running." Gracelia said, swinging the wooden sword at them.

They fell to their knees and groveled for forgiveness and that they'll try harder. Hugh thought back to his wife's words, *'Then you just train her like she's a man, she'll see she can't even compare to the other knights.'* She wasn't like the other knights, she was her own person and was showing it, right in front of him. She was showing a fierceness he hadn't seen since he was a child. "Alright, one more chance or you're both running till midnight!" Gracelia told them, they stood up and showed her the stance again. Hugh smiled as she picked it up and swung her wooden sword as instructed. She was a fast learner soon she was actually beating them at practice swordplay within two hours.

The men huffed as Gracelia landed blow after blow on their knees, thighs and hips. She was small but agile and bested them when they both suddenly collapsed to the ground. "We give! We give!" Gracelia frowned, she was having to much fun beating them up as punishment. She felt alive with the wooden sword in her hands, she enjoyed the rush that she was feeling. She looked down at the two exhausted knights in front of her and huffed at them, before she could say anything her stomach growled, the sun at it's highest peak. She whipped at the sweat on her brow, but she didn't feel exhausted or even a tiny bit winded despite the sun's rays hitting her.

"I need food." She mumbled to herself, she looked around for her father and found him sitting with Sir Lee and smiling as he talked. "Papa!" She yelled running over to him, he turned his head and smiled at her, her hair trailing behind her. "Did you see what I did? Did you?" She placed the wooden sword on the table next to him, a smile plastered on her face.

"Yes I did. You're quite a fast learner my little snowflake." He looked at his daughter and didn't see any sort of exhaustion on her face, he knew his wife wouldn't be happy once he told her how good their daughter was at using a sword, a wooden sword, put a sword nonetheless. Before he could continue he heard her stomach growl, Gracelia's face became as pink as the flowers in the garden. He stood up, the wooden chair creaking and gathered her in his arms. "Shall we eat?" He asked her as they made their way past the other sparring knights. Gracelia nodded her head. He looked over at Sir Lee who was following them five feet behind. "Tell the men to eat and to continue sparing after, I'm gonna spend some time with my daughter." Sir Lee nodded, turned and headed back to the knights.

Gracelia watched as they all sheathed their blades and rejoiced at the concept of a meal, before she could see anything else the door shut behind her, blocking her view of the courtyard.

CHAPTER SIX

Hugh headed towards the dining room door when he saw a knight standing in front of the drawing-room door. "Marquis!" Gracelia called out, waving. The knight turned at the sound of his name and smiled. He looked at the door and walked over to Hugh with his daughter still in his arms.

Marquis kneeled, "Good evening my lord and lady." Hugh waringly looked at the stranger in front of him, pulling his daughter closer to him to protect her.

"Who are you?" Gracelia looked at her father in surprise, feeling his body tense up under her small hand.

"Papa? That's Marquis. He was standing at my door this morning, standing guard." Hugh placed Gracelia down and pushed her behind him. Drawing his sword he put the flat of the blade on the knight's shoulder, threateningly. Marquis looked at Hugh's face, a stone mask devoid of emotion. The young girl stared at the knight, confused at what was happening.

"My lord..."

"DON'T! STATE WHO YOU ARE!" Hugh commanded the young man, drawing his blade closer to the knight's neck.

"My name is Marquis Volvix. The Chancellor of the Highness sent me to watch over you and your family. My orders were to stay inside guard the young mistress and the Duchess, should the need arise." He looked at the stunned face of the young girl behind her father. He didn't want her to see him as a threat but the look in her eyes made him sad. Hugh withdrew his sword from the man's neck with a sigh.

"That damned Marcus! He should have told me first!" He sheathed his sword and put a hand on the knight's shoulder. He wanted to show his daughter that even though he seemed like a threat at first, his actions were because of the orders given. "Next time report first, before inserting yourself in my family's sights. Understood?" Marquis bowed his head.

"Yes, my lord." Hugh motioned for the man to stand, Marquis did.

"From now on, you will guard my daughter at her door and everywhere she goes. Since it seems you've left quite a good impression on her," Hugh motioned to Gracelia. "Introduce yourself, my little snowflake."

"We have already..." Marquis said but Gracelia caught him by surprise. She curtsied as best as she could while wearing pants.

"I am Gracelia Da Mornica, daughter of Duke Hugh Da Mornica. Pleasure to make your acquaintance, knight Marquis." Her hair fell over her shoulders, creating a blanket around her. Marquis smiled and bowed to the young girl.

"The pleasure is all mine, my lady." Marquis looked at the young girl in front of him, not surprised by her attire, since he'd heard the gossip from the kitchen staff when the Duchess came down for breakfast. "My lord." Hugh looked at the knight.

"What is it?"

"The Duchess has a visitor, she's in the drawing-room." Hugh went rigged.

"Grab Gracelia and hold her in your arms," Hugh commanded the knight. "I don't want her wasting any energy on small tasks such as walking until we can go back outside and let her train." Gracelia lifted her arms up to Marquis, he lifted her up and placed her in the crook of his arm.

"Marquis?" The young girl asked.

"Yes, my lady?" He looked at the small girl in his arms.

"Why don't you wear armor like the other knights?" She waved her hand towards the door leading to the courtyard.

"I didn't train for battle, young mistress." Gracelia looked over at him confused.

"I thought all knights trained for battle." Maquis laughed at her causing Gracelia to smack his arm.

"My sincere apologies, my lady. However, some knights are taught to be guards for noble families, we only know the basics to protect those in our charge." Gracelia wanted to ask more but her father opened the door to the drawing-room. Inside there was; a hearth, paintings of flowers and mountains on the walls, a plush couch with two love seats, underneath were carpets thrown over each other to provide cushion under people's feet. On the low table was a white vase that had one rose in it on a tray holding two sets of teacups and a kettle on a purple cloth. Inside was Gracelia's mother on the couch facing the door, on the other was a woman. Gracelia couldn't see her face because her back was to the door. Much to her surprise, Juliana looked at Gracelia in horror. She quickly stood up, trying to hide her shock from the woman.

"Excuse me Liliana. I'll be right back, please enjoy the tea." Juliana told the woman, upon further inspection Gracelia could see that Liliana had light blonde hair that was almost pure white in the sunlight streaming through the window. Hugh sighed as Juliana walked around the loveseats and stood in front of him, pushing him out. Shutting the door behind her, she glared at her husband. "What were you thinking?! If she had seen Gracelia dressed like that the secret would be out!" Juliana was fuming at her husband. Gracelia buried her face in the Knights neck, ashamed and embraced at causing her mother to worry. "You!" She pointed to Marquis. The knight straightened his back.

"Yes, my lady?"

"Take Gracelia to her room, have her dress worthy of her station." Juliana told him, pointing to her daughter, a hint of disgust in her voice as she looked at Gracelia in men's clothing. Marquis bowed his head to her before turning to walk towards the stairs. Gracelia peeked from the knight's neck and saw her mother with her arms crossed over her chest in anger.

~~~~~~~~~

Adelina gracefully weaved Gracelia's curls into a braid down her back, pinning loose hair here and there with white pins. Standing back she admired her handiwork, marveling at the way they wove the sapphire topped pins into the curls. She caught Gracelia's face in the mirror, her eyes shiny. Adelina put her hands on the young girl's shoulders. "Young mistress? Are you all right?" Before she knew it, the tears rolled down her cheeks, leaving a wet trail behind. "Young mistress!" Adelina pulled the chair away from the mirror and knelt in front of the girl, holding Gracelia's hands in hers.

"Mother hates me, doesn't she?" Gracelia asked her nanny in a small voice.

"What? No!" Adelina squeezed the young girl's small hands, worried about what had brought on these thoughts. "Why do you think she hates you?" Gracelia sniffled.

"Mother seemed angry at me earlier..." Gracelia told her, remembering the look of horror on her mother's face. "I was wearing my training attire, and she looked at me as if I wasn't her daughter." Adelina shook her head.

"Oh! Oh, you sweet girl. She doesn't hate you, she's just not used to you becoming so strong. Forgive me for saying this but she's quite set in her ways. According to your father when they first met she wouldn't do anything that will make people think she was not a lady and when he would court her and go on walks, she always had an umbrella with her as if she was afraid that the sun would burn her to a crisp. She always had her hair up, always in a bun or pins. According to the woman in the village she's the perfect image of a noble lady." Adelina said, watching Gracelia's face as the tears dried.

"Thank you, Adelina." Gracelia said with a sad smile.

"Whatever happens, don't give up on what you want young mistress." Adelina knew how to talk to kids with hurt hearts, when her father passed away her brother had cried for days after they buried him. Thanks to the practice on her brother she could calm a crying child. Gracelia looked at herself in the mirror, her white hair pulled away from her face, she was wearing a light blue and black dress. She lifted her head and spoke to herself in the mirror, ignoring Adeline's smile.

"I am a lady and I am strong. I will not bow to the challenge, I will endure. I will prove to mother that I can be both fragile and strong." Gracelia stood and headed to her door for dinner. She was strong and a lady, soon her mother would finally see she was her own person and she forged her own destiny.

CHAPTER SEVEN

December came and Gracelia trained with Tomas and Alexander every day during those days. She was a fast learner, that even her father had given her some advice against her mother's wishes but Gracelia avoided her mother at all costs. She'd go down to the courtyard before her mother would wake up, She'd even gone as far as eating with the other men during lunch, her father didn't seem bothered by it since it seemed to her that he was tired most of the time because he had been sleeping in his office. After the incident with the drawing-room and Gracelia being dressed as a boy, Juliana had kicked Hugh out of their bedroom. When she would hide in her room away from her mother, Marquis and Adelina had kept her company. Marquis had even gone as far as teaching her how to handle an intruder should they come in through her balcony door. He'd play out scenarios with her, advising her how to deal with it in certain ways an intruder would come at her.

During one such session her father had been in the room, overseeing how far his daughter had come from not knowing anything about self defense to mastering it with in days. After they were happy that Gracelia knew how to handle herself, they'd all sit down and enjoy tea together. "Gracelia." Hugh said, still sitting in a plush chair that the maids had brought in for them.

"Yes papa?" Gracelia asked her father, turning

away from Marquis, they were discussing other tactics that she could use to her advantage given her room layout. He waved her over, Gracelia ran over to her father, her white hair flowing behind her like a cape. "Yes?" He pulled Gracelia onto his lap.

"I have something for you." He reached into the inside of his jacket and pulled out a sheathed dagger from one of the pockets. On the hilt was a rainbow moonstone that threw off five colors when the sun hit it. Gracelia gasped and looked at her father in shock.

"It's pretty, are you sure I can have it?" Gracelia looked at the dagger with shaking hands, wanting to hold it in her hand. Hugh smiled at his daughter's hesitance to hold it ,since he saw it as a family heirloom. It was his mother's before giving it to him when she fell ill of tuberculosis, his father had it handmade for her on their wedding day.

"Take it." He grabbed his daughter's small hand and placed it on her palm.

"It's light! How is it so light?" Gracelia grabbed onto the hilt with one hand and it melded perfectly to her hand, the silver cord wrapped around it following the grooves of her small hand. Pulling it slowly out of the sheath she realized someone made it out of a black material. "What is this?" Hugh chuckled.

"It is pure obsidian, my little snowflake. Much stronger than steel but much lighter if crafted correctly." Gracelia eyed the black material that her father called obsidian. "I want you to carry this with

you at all times, the good thing about this sheath,"
He flipped it over to show two leather strips big
enough to tie. "It's much easier to hide with it being
smaller but it can still cause damage, another good
thing about it is that you can hide under your dress
if tied around your thigh. My mother used to wear it
like that, she never had the need for it since she
didn't get out much since she was raising me and
my cousin most of the time." He looked at
Gracelia's face with pride as she realized she could
wear it under her dress.

"Thank you papa! Thank you!" She quickly
sheathed the blade and placed it on the table,
wrapping her arms around his neck. "You'll show
me how to use it won't you? Won't you?!" Hugh
nodded, and she hugged him harder, not wanting to
let go.

~~~~~~~~~~

Gracelia fidgeted in her seat, her plate untouched.
She felt uncomfortable with her mother sitting right
in front of her slowly eating and casting worried
glances at her. Juliana opened her mouth to say
something when a voice broke the silence. "My
lord, a letter from the imperial palace has arrived!"
Hugh placed down his fork when Sir Lee came in,
holding it carefully in his hands. He offered it to
Gracelia's father and bowed, once Hugh grabbed it.

"What is it Hugh? What is it?" Juliana asked,
excited. "Is it a royal summons?"

"Let me open it first, my dear." Hugh said with a
chuckle, he slowly peeled the wax seal and opened

the envelope. Inside was a accede, formally inviting them to the Royal New Year's Ball that the palace has every year. "The Emperor is inviting us to the annual new year's ball this year." Hugh clenched his teeth whereas Juliana screamed in joy.

"Oh, my gosh! Oh, my gosh! Yes, I am so excited!" Juliana looked at Gracelia with a huge smile. "I can get Gracelia a new dress since we still have two weeks before the ball and I can buy new pins for her hair! What if she catches the crowned prince's eye Hugh? That'll be such an honor to our family! I could call the Empress my sister-in-law!" Hugh rubbed his temples, thinking back to the Emperor saying he wanted Gracelia to marry his son.

Gracelia's face drained of color, she'd read that many of the royals were spoiled and snobs who thought them higher that even apologizing was below them. Juliana just smiled throughout the whole meal, whereas Hugh and Gracelia ate in silence listening to the woman ramble on and on about patterns and colors that would look amazing on her daughter's milk white skin. Gracelia touched the dagger on her thigh, comforted at the fact were anything to happen, she could protect herself from any unwanted attention.

CHAPTER EIGHT

"Now announcing Duke and Duchess Da Mornica, and their young daughter!" Gracelia pulled on the collar of her dress nervously. The dark oak wood door opened and they could hear the music, she quickly put her hands on the side of her dress and walked behind her parents. Her father was wearing a dark blue suit with the Da Mornica insignia on the pocket of the jacket, her mother was wearing a light green dress with white beads embroidered into the hem and collar of the dress. The attending guests all gawked as Gracelia came into view, her white hair a stark contrast against the light blue and black dress she was wearing. That's when the whispering started.

"Is that?"

"It is!"

"She's the fabled child?"

"I can see why the rumors say she's pretty."

"Her hair is so unnatural."

"Kinda like fresh snow, don't you agree?"

Gracelia cast her eyes to the ground, embarrassed. A light shade of pink reached her cheeks, her hair up in a bun, with curls hanging out the back. She felt bare because she was showing too much of her neck for her to even feel comfortable surrounded by all the nobles she's never met. Her parents stopped in front of her, Hugh kneeled and Juliana curtsied. Gracelia followed suit when she heard her parents say in unison "May the sun always shine on you, your majesty's." Gracelia looked up from between her parents. The man sitting on the throne in front of them was about the same age as her father. He was also chubby and wearing a red cloak, they could see a black shirt beneath it. He was wearing black pants with red on the hem. His black hair partially hidden underneath his crown, his brown eyes shining with amusement.

"Please rise my old friend!" They all stood, the emperor laughed. "It's good to see you." He turned to the woman on his left. "My dear this is Duke Da Mornica, he fought alongside me during the battle of Blood lake." Gracelia looked over and to her surprise the woman had hair the color of fire, her eyes as black as night. She was wearing a red dress that had a lotus flower stitched near the hem. She smiled at her husband, on her head was a gold circlet with rubies interwoven into the expensive material. Gracelia thought it must weigh a ton, but the empress didn't seem fazed about it at all.

"My dear, he's the fabled black knight?" Gracelia held her breath, it surprised her to hear that coming from the Empress. They called her father the black knight during the days of blood lake, it was said he was ruthless on the battlefield. Hugh coughed in embarrassment and covered his mouth with his hand. The Emperor looked over at Hugh and laughed, smacking his belly.

"My old friend! Don't be embarrassed of that title! You were my right-hand man during those days, we were so young back then but yet it seems like you haven't aged since." Gracelia watched as her father looked away, his face the color of fresh blood. The Emperor noticed and laughed harder. "Dear me Hugh! When did you get so soft!" The Empress chuckled behind her hand that's when she noticed Gracelia and stood in surprise.

"Is that your young daughter? The blessed snow as the temple of the north calls her." The Empress asked, looking at Hugh in amazement. Hugh stepped away from his wife so they could see Gracelia. When she was in view, the Emperor stood up next to his wife. "Dear! She's just as the rumors say. Come here, child." Gracelia hesitated and looked at her father, he nodded his head. She walked towards them and curtsied.

"May the sun always shine on you, your majesty's." Gracelia said, remembering the words her parents had said a few minutes prior. The Empress smiled.

"She's polite and well behaved! Not like other children at all, I remember when Christopher first met the Duke he was so shy and hid behind my dress." The Empress laughed at the memory, it shocked Gracelia at how kind they seemed to be despite the Emperor being called the blood dragon. Gracelia thought back to the history book that Adelina had told her to read. It said people would call the Emperor the blood dragon because of his prowess and strength in battle, it said he could kill a man where he stood. "What's your name, child?" The Empress asked Gracelia, snapping the young girl from her thoughts.

"My name is Gracelia Da Mornica, your highness." Gracelia said still in a curtsy. The Empress clapped her hands together and walked closer, she knelt down and put her hands on Gracelia's dress smoothing the fabric.

"It's a pleasure to meet you, young lady. I hope you enjoy the ball, please have fun." Gracelia looked at the Empress, she was smiling but it didn't reach her eyes. She turned Gracelia around and gasped. "That pin! It's beautiful!" Underneath the bun was the pin she had gotten from her father. "May I ask where did you get it?" Hugh came forward and put his hand on his daughter's shoulder.

"We got it from our black smith, your grace. He's rather skilled in the art of forging metal into beautiful pieces."

"You must let me meet him! I'd love for a new pin myself!" The Empress told Hugh with excitement. She looked around at all the nobles staring at her in awe, she straightened herself and brushed off her dress. "My apologies, please, enjoy the ball!" She went back to her seat and watched as Hugh led his daughter to a group he recognized. Her eyes never leaving the snowflake pin.

~~~~~~~~

Gracelia looked around the hall, watching children run between groups of people, laughing. She didn't see the point in running around during a ball where ladies and nobles were dancing. She looked up at her parents; they were too busy talking and laughing to realize if she left. She slowly walked away from her parents and towards an open window. She stopped and breathed in the winter air. Her eyes flashing over the trees and rested on the town below the palace. People were running about, celebrating the coming of the new year. Gracelia sighed and took it all in, she's never been to the royal Palace and was in awe of all the buildings she could see.

"Good Evening." She turned and saw Nicholas standing beside her wearing a suit with the rune family crest on his suit pocket.

"Good Evening, Nicholas." She said back in a less than friendly tone.

"About the library that day..." Nicholas rubbed the back of his neck, looking anywhere but at her.

"What about it?" Gracelia asked him, she turned back towards the window wishing he'd go away.

"I'm deeply sorry for what I said during our meeting that day. I didn't realize that your father was a close friend to the Emperor." Nicholas looked at her waiting for an answer but all he got was a laugh.

"You're surely kidding?" Gracelia laughed, Nicholas looked at her in shock.

"I... I am most certainly not kidding, Lady Gracelia." She stiffened at being called lady but then relaxed remembering that she was still a girl. "I have someone who wishes to meet you." Gracelia turned and looked at him.

"Who might that be?" She asked him.

"That would be me." She followed the voice behind Nicholas and gasped. Behind him stood a boy with maroon colored hair and brown eyes, he was wearing a red suit with gold trimmings around the collar and at the end of his sleeves. Nicholas fidgeted and waved his hand towards the boy who couldn't have been but eleven.

"This is..." Nicholas started to say before being cut off by the boy.

"I am Christopher Marksman, the crowned prince and future Emperor of this land." Gracelia looked at the boy in shock.

"The... the crowned prince?" She couldn't believe what she was seeing.

CHAPTER NINE

Christopher laughed at Gracelia's expression and walked closer to her, pushing Nicholas aside. He leaned down and put his face close to hers, his breath smelled of juniper berries. "Are you that shocked? Have you not heard of me?" He asked her, amused at her silence. Gracelia stepped back and curtsied.

"May the sun always shine on you, your highness." Gracelia said, wishing he wasn't so close to her. He put his hand on her head and laughed. "You're rather short for a seven-year-old. When I was your age I was taller than an oak sapling." He lifted his hand and put his fingers under her chin lifting her face to look at his. "Your eyes are a rather surprising color. How would I describe them..." Gracelia felt her face grow hot under his gaze and quickly stood up and stepped away, dislodging his finger from under her chin, He snapped his fingers, ignoring her movement while trying to think. "Sapphires! That's how I'd describe your eyes!" He pointed his finger at her and laughed. "You have jewel eyes but you're no jewel. I've seen girls much prettier than you up north." Gracelia bit the inside of her cheek to keep from yelling at him for his rude comment. "What was your name again?" Gracelia's jaw dropped, he wanted to meet her but forgot her name.

"She is Gracelia Da Mornica, your Highness."

Nicholas said walking up behind Christopher. Christopher looked at her in amusement.

"Will you take a walk with me? It's to stuffy in this ballroom." He walked past Gracelia not giving her time to answer and didn't turn to see if she was following. Gracelia thought for a moment but followed him, knowing it would cause her mother to be angry at her for refusing. They walked through an open door and out into the palace garden. "This is my favorite place to go when I need to be alone, to bad all the flowers have died and the trees have lost their leaves. Usually, it's beautiful but now it looks like a dead forest." He looked around and laughed. "At least the bushes are still alive..." Before he could say anything else, Gracelia felt a sharp prick on her neck. The Prince looked at Gracelia in surprise but it wasn't at Gracelia but at a man in black behind her, holding a knife to her neck.

"Move and she dies." Gracelia went rigged at the voice, it was deep and gruff. "I came here for you dear prince, someone has paid a high price for your head." The Prince just stared at the man not saying anything, his hand twitched at his side. "I told you don't..." Before he could say anything else Gracelia quickly hiked up her dress and found the hilt of the knife on her thigh, she took it out of its sheath and stomped on the man's foot, causing him to grunt in pain. She spun on her heels and plunged the dagger into his side, the black figure looked at her in surprise, his hands went for his side as he fell to his knees. She took out the dagger and plunged it into the side of his neck breaking his major artery. She turned his head with one hand and yanked out the dagger, causing the blood vessel to spray blood onto her face and dress. She watched as his body convulsed, blood spilling from his neck onto the ground.

"Someone has attacked the Prince!" Gracelia heard someone say, she looked up from the dead body as royal guards came into view. They gasped as they saw her covered in blood.

"Seize her!" Yelled one guard, but the prince was quickly in front of her covering her with his body.

"She did nothing wrong! She saved me!" He turned his head and saw that Gracelia's eyes were nothing more than dark blue pools of emotions. What he saw scared him, he didn't see fear or sadness. He took a step away from her in fear. Hugh pushed the royal guards aside and ran to his daughter, yanking a handkerchief from his pocket and wiped at her face as he kneeled down in front of her.

"Gracelia? My little snowflake, are you all right?" He asked, looking at her in worry.

"Papa?" She finally said, the dagger fell from her hands and onto the cobblestone. He quickly picked it up and folded it into the handkerchief and placed it in his pocket.

"It's ok my little snowflake." He looked over at the body with surprise, she had gone after the areas on a man's body to cause pain before killing him.

"Where is she? Is my little girl alright? Gods please let her be alright!" Juliana yelled from behind the guards.

"Juliana! She's all right!" Hugh called out to her. "Let her through!" The guards let Juliana through and she ran to her husband and daughter. "Gracelia! My baby!" She put her hands on her daughter's shoulders and looked at her dress. "She's covered in blood! Get a doctor!" Then she felt a warm soft hand on her face.

"It's not mine mama. It's his." She pointed to the dead body beside her, Juliana looked over and screamed in horror.

~~~~~~

They had canceled the ball until tomorrow when the feast would begin. Gracelia looked out the window, her hair wet from the bath the royal maids had given her, the door opened but she paid it no mind. "Gracelia, are you alright?" Hugh asked his daughter. He closed the door behind him and walked towards her, placing a hand on the top of her head. "You did good." Gracelia looked at her father in the window.

"I did what had to..." She told her father. "I had to ... right?" Her voice shook at the end. Hugh wrapped his arms around her tiny shoulders, she was shaking.

"Yes. Yes you did my sweet strong girl." Gracelia turned her body and put her face in his chest, tears streamed down her face. "You protected yourself. I'm sorry I wasn't there to protect you. I'm so sorry, my little snowflake." Hugh told her crying, he buried his face in her hair and cried softly. He felt guilty for not being there and that she had to take her first life in a place that was swarming with guards. Once she had stopped shaking, she pulled away and put her hand on her father's face.

"It's not your fault, you can't be there for me every minute of every day. I'm just glad you taught me how to protect myself papa." He fell to his knees in front of his daughter and pulled her to him, resting his head on her shoulder.

"I'm sorry you had to take your first life my little girl, my sweet baby." His body shook again. She wrapped her arms around his neck and played with his hair as he cried. She was angry but more at the fact that the prince didn't say anything at all, but she was proud for showing the snobby prince that she can protect herself if need be. However, her mother wasn't happy.

CHAPTER TEN

"Your highness, I am deeply sorry for my
daughter's conduct last night in front of the prince."
Juliana told the Empress as she sent a sideways
glance to her daughter who was sitting on the chair
between them. Gracelia sat silently, her eyes on her
hands. She hated the dress she was wearing, it was
above her knees and her hair was in braids to show
innocence. She hated the color pink, and she wanted
nothing more than to run back to her room the
Emperor had given her. "We had given her the
dagger she used for her birthday because she
thought it was pretty." The Empress looked down at
the obsidian dagger in front of her on the table. She
noticed that it was clean of any blood and shined in
the light from the window, causing the rainbow
moonstone to cast colors onto the table.

The Empress leaned forward and grasped the
small thing in her hand. She eyed it, it was much
too small for her hands and she couldn't see how the
small girl she'd met last night had used it. She
looked back up at Juliana.

"What does your daughter have to say in this
matter?" Juliana looked over at Gracelia.

"Gracelia!" Her daughter's head snapped up in
shock.

"Y... yes mother?" She said in a small voice.
"What do you have to say to the Empress?" Juliana
glared at her daughter, watching her every move.
Gracelia got out of her seat and knelt on the floor

beside the Empress, like her mother had told her to do before they had arrived.

"I am very sorry for my conduct, your majesty. I had forgotten that I had it on me." She put her hands on the floor and touched her head between them in a formal bow of forgiveness. "I enjoy having it on me because when light touches the stone it casts off pretty colors." Gracelia cringed at her own words, she sounded weak and she hated it. The Empress laughed and covered her mouth with her hand.

"Dear me! The shock must have made your age go backwards child." Juliana looked at the Empress in surprise. "Don't reply with what your mother told you to say, child. You enjoyed it didn't you? Being strong?" Gracelia snapped her head up at the Empresses choice of words before she could reply, Juliana cut her off.

"Your highness! She's a child, and she's a girl! I mean a girl needs to be sweet and weak." The Empress smacked her hand on the table, making them all jump. The dagger stayed planted, not moving under the weight of the Empress' hand. "You forget your place, Lady Juliana. I am speaking to your daughter, you will keep your mouth shut! I am being lenient in letting you stay as I speak with your daughter. If you do not agree to what I have to say you may leave!" Juliana cringed and put her hands on her lap. "Good." She turned to Gracelia. "Goodness child, get up and sit next to me." Gracelia was grateful as the Empress helped her stand and patted the seat next to her. She sat down and stared at the dagger. "Now tell me, what is it that is so important about the dagger." Gracelia looked at her mother, wondering what to say. Juliana stared at Gracelia, her eyes telling to keep to the story. The Empress put her hand on Gracelia's cheek and made the young girl look at her. "Ignore your mother and tell me the truth." Gracelia swallowed.

"I enjoy having it because it makes me feel strong. My dream is to be the first female knight and protect those I love your majesty. My father gave me the dagger as a gift when I had finished the basics." The Empress looked at the young girl in surprise.

"You trained for how long?" She asked her, intrigued.

"When I turned seven." The Empress almost laughed.

"You're saying that you trained almost a month ago and you're already using a real weapon?"

"Yes, your Majesty." The Empress looked taken by surprise at the young girl's words. She looked over at the child's mother, she didn't seem to happy about what Gracelia had told her.

"You didn't agree to the training I suppose, Lady Juliana?"

"No, your majesty! My husband and I had an agreement, he would train her like a man in order for her to quit. I didn't agree on it going as far as her using a real weapon." The Empress just looked at Juliana in surprise and shock.

"You're saying that you don't want your daughter to follow her dream? To grow up and be like you?" The Empress challenged.

"N... No your majesty! I wanted her to grow up as a lady and to make her father and I proud." The Empress sighed and caught the sad look on Gracelia's face at her mother's words.

"She is a lady, her court etiquette is better than most girls her age, that is something to be proud of Lady Juliana. Let her train to become a knight, she'll still be a lady out of armor or training clothing. Her manners and knowledge is astonishing at this age. When I was her age, I only played with dolls and never knew how to hold myself in front of those higher ranking." She put her hand around Graciela's and grabbed the dagger from the table. "This is yours and it shall remain yours under my royal command. I will send the best royal trainer we have to your home after the new year celebration." Gracelia looked up at the Empress in shock, she bent down and kissed the young girl's forehead. "You are strong and you will show all these people that doubt you, show them you can be both a lady and a knight in this cruel world of ours. Thank you for protecting my son, lady Gracelia, I am forever in your debt." She pulled away from the young girl and stood up. "You will train with my son today, make sure your ready before I have to send someone to fetch you."

The Empress gathered her skirts and headed to the door, her read hair swinging. She looked back at the mother and daughter. "Be proud Juliana, I would be if she were my daughter." After speaking she left, Gracelia watched her leave in awe.

~~~~~~~~

Gracelia skipped happily beside her mother, excited to be training with the royal guard. "Gracelia..." Juliana said under her breath, Gracelia turned with a smile. Juliana raised her hand and slapped her daughter causing her to fall to the ground, the dagger falling from her hand. Gracelia looked up at her mother, her hand on her cheek. Juliana had tears in her eyes, her face red in anger. She turned and walked away leaving her daughter sitting there staring after her. Gracelia sat there in shock, watching the dagger slowly spin till it stopped. Her hand still on her cheek.

"What did I do?" She asked herself, her mother had never raised a hand against her before. She slowly stood up and brushed off her dress, she slowly touched her cheek and winced. She went over to the dagger and went to go pick it up when a voice stopped her.

"Make way for the Emperor!" Gracelia stood up with the dagger in hand, she held it behind her back. The emperor was in eyesight when she curtsied.

"Good morning your highness!" Gracelia said, trying to hide the mark on her cheek. The Emperor looked over at her voice.

"AH! Lady Gracelia! How are you this morning? I hope the talk with my wife went well?" He asked her, stopping in front of her.

"Yes, your majesty, all is well." She told him, head still down. The Emperor looked at her with worry. He put his hand on her cheek and she winced, pulling away.

"You dare move away from the Emperor?" Said one of the royal guards, the Emperor put up his hand.

"Wait! Lady Gracelia, lift your head." She slowly lifted her head and the Emperor gasped and put his hands on her shoulders. "What happened? Who did this?" He touched the mark on her cheek softly as to not hurt her. He looked at the guards. "Find whoever did this! Who dare touch the daughter of the Emperors' friend?" He yelled, still holding onto Gracelia's shoulders.

"Your majesty..." She said in a soft voice, he turned his head to look at the young girl in front of him.

"What is it Lady Gracelia?" He asked in worry.

"Please don't worry about it..." He looked at her in surprise.

"How can I not! You are the daughter of my good friend Hugh! Whoever dares to raise a hand against you just harmed your father's honor!" Gracelia flinched at his words, she didn't want her mom to be in trouble.

"Please, you're highness. I just want to see my father." She said softly. The Emperor grabbed her hand.

"Where is lady Gracelia's father?"

"In the Library, your grace." The Emperor pulled

Gracelia with him as he made his way to the library, angry at whoever dared touch the young girl beside him.

CHAPTER ELEVEN

They stopped at a wooden door and in front of it were two royal guards. "The Royal Emperor is entering the library!" Called a guard to the door, it opened and Gracelia saw the royal library for the first time. She gasped at the floor to ceiling bookshelves in surprise, wondering how long it'd take her to read every book. Her eyes stopped on her father, he was coming towards them, the Emperor pulled her along and the door shut behind them. She let go of the Emperor's hand and ran towards her father.

"Papa!!!" She yelled, arms held out to him, he smiled and kneeled down as she ran into his arms. "Hello, my little snowflake." He held her out at arms' length and looked at the dress in disgust. "Pink is not your color, my sweet girl." He looked at her face and gasped at the red mark on her cheek. "Gracelia? Who did this?" He asked her, his hand gently caressing her cheek. His daughter looked down. not saying anything.

"I was hoping you could answer that for me Hugh." The Emperor told the girl's father. "I found her like that and she was all alone standing in the hallway." Hugh looked at his daughter in shock, worried about however had hit her in the royal palace.

"You still have the dagger, don't you?" Gracelia nodded. 'Whoever did it wasn't a threat immediately or she would have used the dagger.' He thought to himself. "Let me talk with my daughter privately.

Excuse us, your majesty." He said as he led Gracelia to a window seat in the corner of the room. He sat her down and put his hands on her knees, kneeling in front of her. "Who did this to you? Was it the Empress?" Gracelia shook her head.

"No, papa." Hugh held his daughter's hand.

"Then who?" He asked her, worried. Gracelia bit her lip and fidgeted in her seat. She leaned forward and whispered in her father's ear.

"It was mama." She pulled away and looked at Hugh, pleadingly. "Don't tell the Emperor, please papa." She whispered to her father, squeezing his hand in hers.

"So? Any luck Hugh?" The Emperor asked him, walking over. "Find out who did that to her?"

"No, your majesty. She said she must have hurt herself in her sleep." He told the man, feeling guilty for lying to his friend. The Emperor rubbed his face with his hand.

"Please Hugh, enough with the formalities. We went to war together, call me by my first name." Hugh clenched his jaw and looked to see that the guards had left the room while he was talking to his daughter, the Emperor caught on and laughed. "We're alone, in private don't be so formal."

"Yes, your maj.... I mean yes Aland." Hugh said, looking up at his war buddy.

"Your highness?" Gracelia asked, looking at Aland.

"Yes, Lady Gracelia?"

"What does your name mean? I read that most

royals names mean something." Hugh looked at his daughter and smiled.

"Well, it means bright as the sun." Aland told the young girl, Gracelia snapped her fingers.

"That's why we greet you that way!" She said in amazement. Aland laughed and put his hand on Hugh's shoulder.

"You have one smart daughter, my friend." Hugh smiled at his praise.

"Thank you Aland. She spent most of her time in the library when she was five." Gracelia smiled and giggled. Hugh looked at his daughter's cheek in sadness, conflicted over what to do about his wife.

~~~~~~~~~

Hugh looked at his wife in anger as he watched the maids do her hair for the feast. Once they had finished they left, leaving him alone with Juliana. "We need to talk Juliana." Hugh told her, trying to control his anger.

"What about my dear?" She asked not looking at him, she was fixing her earrings.

"About what you did." His voice trailed off as his wife turned to him, her face showing no emotion.

"I don't understand." She got up from her seat and walked over to him, she reached for his hand.

"You already know Juliana." He told her, taking a step away from her. She looked at him dumbfounded, crossing her arms over her chest.

"What in God's name are you getting at?" Juliana's eyes became hard, showing no emotion while waiting for his answer.

"Gracelia..." Her name came off his lips like a blessing, his fatherly love dripping from his voice. Juliana laughed and covered her mouth with her hand.

"Oh! Her!" Hugh looked at her in shock, he saw nothing of the women he'd fallen in love with in front of him. She was drunk off the power she felt in the Palace. She knew she was in higher standing than any of the other nobles.

"What do you mean? HER? She's our daughter Juliana! Call her by the name you gave her when you held her in your arms seven years ago!" Hugh clenched his fist in anger, staring at his wife. She met his gaze, not cowering under it.

"She's more like your daughter than mine Hugh. I see that now, you took her away from me." Juliana challenged him to say otherwise.

"SHE is your daughter to Juliana! WE both raised her! TOGETHER or did you forget that?" Hugh challenged, he would not back down just to please his wife.

"You seem to have forgotten who she holds the closest to her heart, my DEAR." She said the word dear like poison, she wanted her words to feel like venom in her husband's ears.

"You are NOT the woman I fell in love with Juliana! What happened to the woman who cared about her daughter?" Juliana took a step back in surprise.

"You dare say I don't care! I care about her! You're the one who doesn't seem to care! You're

71

training her to be a KNIGHT! The most dangerous job in this era Hugh! Or did you forget what you saw during that war?" Hugh cringed back from her words, remembering the blood on his face, watching it drip from his blade. In front of him, a child lay dying at his feet.

"T...That's not fair! I didn't know he was a kid Juliana! He was wearing a knight's armor!"

"Yet, you still didn't save him." She told him, her words hitting his heart like a dagger. She wasn't wrong, he was too drunk on power then.

"I vowed at your feet! I promised that I would never become that monster again!" Juliana laughed at his pain.

"You will still and forever be the blooded black knight my dear husband. Best remember what you're sending our daughter off to. From what I saw and heard from the Prince, we're already at the brink of another war." She gathered her skirts and turned towards the door. "I'll see you at the feast, my husband." She opened the door and left the room laughing. Hugh collapsed to the floor and punched the carpet in anger. Tears pricked at the back of his eyes.

"Damn you, Juliana." He said, looking at the door as it closed, he heard the latch catch like his own mind was locking him in his memories of the Blood war.

~~~~~~~

That's how Gracelia found him, sitting on the floor with his head down. "Papa?" She asked, closing the door behind her. She carefully walked towards him, worry on her face. She came to a stop and put her hand on his head. Hugh shifted beneath her touch. "Papa..." She said before a hand was around her throat, cutting off her air supply. She looked at her father in horror, his eyes showing nothing of what he was thinking. She struggled in his hold, scratching at his arm. Fear gripped her heart at the thought of dying by her own father's hands. When suddenly his hold on her loosened, she collapsed to the ground, her hands wrapped around her throat trying to breathe.

"Gracelia?" Hugh said, shaking his head. He gasped and moved towards his daughter. She moved away in fear and he stopped, he looked at his hands they were around his daughter's throat only a minute prior. "Gracelia, I am so sorry! My little snowflake please forgive me! I... I didn't know what came over me, I... I wasn't myself!" He stammered trying to remember when he blacked out, but the only memory he could recall was of his wife leaving the room and her harsh words still ringing in his ears playing like a broken record. Gracelia coughed, breaking him from his thoughts.

"It's... ok... papa..." She said between coughs. "I'm... ok... just... need... to... catch... my... breath." She looked up at her father's worried face, smiling sadly at him.

"If you hate me for what I did Gracelia, I completely understand." He told his daughter, feeling guilty at what he'd just done to his fragile snowflake. Gracelia crawled over to him, breathing hard and climbed into his lap. He wrapped his arms around her, pulling her tightly against him. "What did I do to deserve a daughter like you?" He asked the surrounding air.

"I love you papa." Gracelia told him, her head in his chest. Coughs still raked her tiny body but she could breathe. He put his face in her hair and pulled her tighter to him. "Can't breathe, squeezing too hard." Hugh loosened his grip.

"Sorry! I'm sorry!" Gracelia looked up at her father and put her hand on his cheek with a smile.

"It's ok papa, I want you to be ok." Hugh touched her hand on his cheek. He stared down at his daughter in his lap. Her eyes filled with love, no hatred or anger. He sighed in relief and brushed a strand of hair from her forehead.

"You are my light in this dark world Gracelia. You are my most prized treasure, no money or title could make me not want you near my side forever." He told his little snowflake, tears filling his eyes. Gracelia looked at her father in surprise, she put her face in his chest as tears fell down her face.

"Thank you, papa." Hugh chuckled as the tears fell down his face. He hugged his daughter, she was his whole world and he would do anything to protect her even if it meant losing the one he use to cherish the most.

CHAPTER TWELVE

Laughter and gossip filled the palace as the feast began. To Aland's dismay Hugh and Gracelia were not in attendance, he looked over at Juliana. She was smiling and laughing with another duchess from the southern region. He heard the door open; he was happy to see his friend and the young snow haired girl. His face fell when he realized they weren't smiling, Gracelia seemed nervous and Hugh had a hard look on his face. He tapped his foot nervously and watched as they came closer. They stopped in front of him and bowed. "May the sun always shine on you, your majesties." They both told them in unison. Aland stood and walked over to his friend, he put his hands on Hugh's shoulders as he straightened.

"Is everything alright?" Aland asked him, curiously. Hugh looked down at Gracelia, she was fidgeting nervously under her mother's gaze.

"May we speak in private your majesty?" Hugh asked Aland, Gracelia had convinced him to tell Aland what Juliana had done and how she was behaving. If anyone could make her change, it would be the Emperor himself. Aland nodded his head and looked at his wife.

"Mazie, I'll be right back. Enjoy the feast my love." The Empress smiled at her husband and waved him away. "This way, we will talk in the royal parlor." Aland told them while walking away from the pair and to a nearby door. Hugh grabbed

onto Gracelia's hand and followed the Emperor.
They entered a well lit room, a slight breeze rustled
the curtains from the half-opened window. Inside
someone had arranged plush red couches to be in
front of each other, red candles were on the coffee
table. Hanging on the walls were paintings of past
Emperor's. Aland smiled at Gracelia's amazement at
the decor. "Now what's going on Hugh?" He asked
his old friend, Aland walked over to one couch and
sat down. He waved his hand at the other. "Please,
sit down." Hugh dragged Gracelia over to the other
couch and sat down.

"Well, your Majesty..." Hugh started.

"Hugh, how many times must I tell you, in
private call me by my first name?" Hugh coughed in
embarrassment.

"I deeply apologize Aland."

"What's going on?" Aland asked Hugh again,
becoming impatient.

"I would like your advice about something." So
Hugh told him about how Juliana had been the one
that slapped Gracelia and how Juliana started to act
differently when they entered the palace, he
explained to Aland that it all started when Gracelia
had protected the crowned prince. Aland listened to
his friend, watching Gracelia slowly crawl into her
own mind for protection. His eyes widened as he
saw the young girl's eyes turn ever darker, what was
once full of life seemed hard and lethal. "That has
happened in the past twenty-four hours." Aland
moved his gaze over to Hugh and saw his friend's

eyes had also become dark pools of nothing. Aland
rubbed his face with his hand sighing.

"It seems she has forgotten her place my friend.
I'm not sure what to tell you, if she were my wife I'd
already have her imprisoned for hurting your
daughter and your own honor. It doesn't matter how
her father raised her, as a duchess she must carry
herself not act like a spoiled rotten child. I see
nothing wrong with Gracelia trying to become a
knight, it won't be easy but she seems like a strong
and capable young girl." His eyes gravitating back
to the young girl seated in front of him. Her eyes
were still dark pools of emotions and for the first
time in his life, he worried about what would
happen if she were to fight on the battlefield.

He'd only seen that look once before today, his
mind traveled back to the Blood War and how Hugh
had that same look before a battle that could turn
the tides to their favor. He remembered the blood
red sand and how it seemed to glisten under his feet
as the sun rose. "Blood red sand can not be stained
if it's already been tainted." He told Hugh,
remembering the saying he had heard from a fellow
knight during that moment. Hugh looked at Aland
in surprise, he knew what the man in front of him
was trying to say.

"You surely don't mean?" Hugh asked his friend,
Aland just stared at him, his eyes not moving.
"Aland, you really think that is the best course of
action? We are no longer at war ,my friend."

"Sometimes the worst war is those that we have

inside ourselves Hugh. Those never truly end until one stands victorious over the other." Aland motioned to Gracelia. "She has her own war brewing in her mind already. Will she fall to it or will you help her stand above it?"

~~~~~~~~

The Empress sat in her seat, listening to the gentle banter of husbands with their wives. She sighed and looked at the door her husband had disappeared into. She slowly rose from her seat and headed towards the door. "Your grace." She stopped and looked over at the voice. Much to her distaste Juliana was coming towards her, wearing a dress that seemed almost a size to big. Once Gracelia's mother was in front of her, she curtsied. "May the sun always shine on you, your majesty."

"Thank you, lady Juliana. Are you finding the feast to your liking?" The Empress asked the woman, wishing she'd leave her be.

"The food is amazing, the aromas are exquisite and pleasant to breathe your grace..." The Empress rolled her eyes as the woman in front of her kept talking when she finally saw her escape. She acted as if she would faint when Juliana put her hands on her arms. "Your grace! Are you alright?" The Empress internally smiled at her acting.

"I'm sorry, lady Juliana, I must have eaten too much. I'm going to the parlor to rest, please excuse me." She gently moved her arms out of the woman's grasp and opened the door to the parlor, smiling as Mazelina left Juliana standing there, stunned into silence.

"I'm not sure what I can do Aland..." The Empress heard someone say, she silently made her way towards the voice.

"Aland, is everything alright, my dear?" She asked Aland as the three came into view. She smiled at her husband, his eyes filled with love.

"Mazelina, my dear! What are you doing here? Is everything all right?" Mazelina laughed at her husband, out of the corner of her eye she saw Hugh stand.

"Please, don't get up. Did I interrupt an important matter?" She looked over at the small child still sitting on the couch not moving. "Is Lady Gracelia alright?" Mazelina asked, quickly heading over to the young girl. She kneeled in front of Gracelia and put her hands on the girl's knees. "Gracelia?" She shook the young girl softly that's when she noticed the girl's eyes were darker than they usually were. "What happened? Do I need to call the doctor?" Aland shook his head and Hugh looked away.

"No my love, she's protecting herself."

"Protecting herself? From what?" Mazelina asked them, becoming angry. "What has happened for her to become like this?" That's when Hugh jumped back into explaining everything that had happened. Mazelina's emotions became more active at every word he spoke, until she felt like a volcano about to erupt.

"That has happened, your grace." Mazelina stood up and threw her hands into the air.

"That stupid, idiotic little wench! She thinks she can do this," She pointed to Gracelia, who was still sitting quietly, locked in her own mind. "To her own daughter and get away with it! I think not! I want her beheaded for the crime of cruelty and greed against her own blood." Aland watched his wife in amazement.

"My love, you can't..." Mazelina looked at him, her eyes ablaze with anger.

"She's lucky this isn't the southern kingdom! She'd already be dead if she lived there, the blood red sand would make it seem like nothing had happened at all." Mazelina paced the room, her arms over her chest in thought.

"My love, calm down, please. It's not beneficial to your health, you know you get sick when angry." Aland told her strolling over to her. She turned and looked at the young girl on the couch, her white hair sticking to the tears that seemed to have fallen from her eyes.

"Gracelia!" Mazelina called to the young girl, she rushed over to her and knelt in front of her. Her fingers whipping away the water droplets on her face. "Wake up child, it's time to come out of that pretty little head of yours." She snapped her fingers near the young girl's ear and a small sound escaped from the girl's lips.

"Your grace?" Mazelina smiled at the young girl, watching her eyes turn back into the sapphire blue she was used to.

"Hello Lady Gracelia." Mazelina told the small

girl in front of her, she reached out her arms and the young girl threw herself into them. Gracelia wrapped her arms around the Empress' neck and cried into her shoulder, letting all the pain leave from her mind. "Shh, it's all right sweet girl. I'm here." Mazelina said rubbing the young girl's head, she kissed the top of Gracelia's head with a smile. "You know who deserves to hurt for what she's caused this young girl to go through. If you do not, you will seek the company of your concubines for the rest of your days." Mazelina glared at Aland as all the color drained from his face at her words. "Guards! Bring Duchess Juliana here now!" Aland yelled at the door leading to the hallway to the royal bedrooms.

"I'm taking lady Gracelia to my room to wash up and sleep, have a maid bring food to my room." Mazelina told her husband, she looked at Hugh. "She'll be in my care, so do not worry Duke Da Mornica." Hugh bowed his head to her.

"Thank you, your grace." He lifted his head and touched his daughter's back. "It will be alright, my little snowflake." Mazelina smiled and headed for the door her husband had just called too when another door opened and a voice was shouting.

"Unhand me! What are you doing?" The Empress quickly stifled a laugh at the desperation in Juliana's voice, happy that they will be rid of her soon enough. She held Gracelia to her chest and made her way to her bedroom, not wanting the child to hear what was surely coming

81

CHAPTER THIRTEEN

Juliana struggled against the guards holding her, they had taken her from the feast in front of all the other nobles. She was furious and angry, wanting to know just what was going on when her husband came into view. She looked around the royal parlor for her daughter but she was not in attendance. "I should have known it was you, my dear husband!" She snapped at him, he didn't flinch at her words.

"I was the one who had you brought here, Lady Juliana." She turned to the voice, Aland was leaning up against the opened window. The breeze ruffling his hair as the curtains swayed with it, almost seeming alive as it twisted and turned in on itself. Juliana quickly curtsied to Aland, she pushed her emotions down, her face becoming a mask of no emotion.

"May the sun always shine on you, your majesty." She told him, her brown hair sticking to her sweat-drenched face.

"You may rise, Lady Juliana." She straightened her back, rubbing her hands on the skirt of her dress, erasing all the creases on the dress her hands had created in the delicate fabric. "Do you know why I had you brought here, Lady Juliana?" Aland asked her, his eyes not giving away anything he was feeling towards her.

"No your grace, I do not." Juliana told him, she watched Hugh's expressionless face from the corner of her eye. He wasn't giving anything away why the royal guards had brought her to the royal parlor. Aland covered his mouth and grinned behind his hand.

"I see, well it's a matter of great importance that was just recently brought to my attention." Aland took his hand away from his face and crossed his arms over his chest. "It seems you have forgotten your place Juliana. You came from a house that once betrayed the emperor prior. I looked into the matter of your upbringing after I found your daughter alone in the hallway this morning with a bruise on her cheek. What I found disturbed me greatly that your father helped hide spies during the Blood war. I would have overlooked it at first seeing as you are the wife to my beloved friend, but after what I've heard today I can not let you behave in such a manner." Juliana gasped, her stone mask falling away.

"Your majesty! I was the one who told the Emperor prior about my father's dealings with the southern region during the war! I have been nothing but a loyal citizen to you and the Empress." Juliana pleaded, her hands resting on her heart as her mind raced. Tears pricked at the back of her eyes, threatening to overwhelm her. "Please your majesty!"

"Lady Juliana, what have you to say against the allegations against you brought by your very own husband and child? I sat there," Aland pointed to one couch. "And watched your child cry into my wife's arms, you broke her while she was trying to please you. Instead of rewarding her, you slapped her and then attacked your husband's honor by bringing up a memory that even I know is too cruel to even talk about. You belittled him, even though he married you against my wishes I might add," He looked at Hugh as if to make a point. "then you do this to your own family? You have no good bone in your body."

"Your majesty, Please!" Juliana fell to the floor, tears fell down her face creating wet streaks in her makeup. "I am just stressed, all I wanted was for my daughter to grow up and be a lady to make her father and I proud. If trying to be a good mother makes me guilty of a crime, then so be it. I did what I could to make her into a young woman who would bring honor to the family. She is corrupted and tainted by tales of heroes and glory from battle. If anyone is to blame, it is her nanny Adelina and her own father for making her believe fairy tales that will never happen for her. For her to be a knight it isn't fit for someone of her status, it is not right." She stated to Aland, trying to do anything to keep from being seen as the bad person in the battle between her husband and the Emperor.

"I sentence you to a year imprisonment until we can hold a convening of nobles to decide your fate. Consider yourself lucky Juliana, you are hereby stripped of the title of lady and must remain imprisoned until the convening. My wife wanted you beheaded Juliana, may the Gods look over you and save you from damnation. Guards! Take her away!" Juliana felt hands around her arms as they jerked her backwards off her legs.

"Hugh! Your majesty, please! I'm sorry! Don't do this!" She looked at Hugh as they dragged her away. "My love! Help me!" Hugh turned his back to her as she screamed, trying to tear away from the guards. They heard the door close, and all was silent, only the rustling of the curtains remained.

~~~~~~~~~

One year later...

"Hah!" Gracelia lunged toward Marquis, he stepped to the side and she turned on her heels smacking his stomach with the flat side of the wooden sword. He groaned but straightened.

"Again!" A male voice called out from behind her, she turned towards Marquis, excited to be sparing with him. Sweat dripped down her brow as the hot sun hit her face. She took her stance and readied herself to attack again. "Start!" She lunged at Marquis again, the flat side of his sword coming up to protect his stomach from her blow. She quickly spun around him, her braid swinging wildly behind her as she moved and placed the tip of the fake sword in the middle of his back.

"Dead." She told Marquis, whipping the sweat from her face with a gloved hand. Marquis turned and smiled down at her. That's when the same man clapped as he walked up to them.

"Well done, Lady Gracelia and you as well Marquis." He said, coming to a stop in front of the two. Gracelia bowed her head in respect and Marquis followed suit.

"Thank you, Sir Michael." They both said in unison, the man's head flew back as he laughed, his brown curly hair streaked with gray shone in the sunlight. His chocolate brown eyes lit up in amusement as he looked at her.

"You've come far in this past year my lady. Seems all the times you've spent out here by yourself seems to have paid off. It's remarkable that only at the age of eight you are showing immense strength many don't show till later training." The compliment made her smile at Michael. Marquis watched the young girl's face brighten, his hands quivered at his sides. He wanted to pat her head and tell her she did a good job but knew he couldn't do that without incurring wrath from her father.

"It was only thanks to your teaching sir Michael. For that I am grateful!" She bowed her head again.

"It..." Michael started to say before a voice cut him off.

"Young mistress! Your father is back!" Gracelia quickly turned towards the voice, running towards them was her nanny. Adelina's brown hair flowing behind her freely, flapping in the wind as she ran. "He's back! The Duke is back!" Gracelia quickly ran towards the woman, grabbing her hand to stop her.

"He's back? He's back?!" Gracelia yelled excited. "Then let's go!" She tightened her grip on the woman's hand and dragged Adelina with her. They quickly entered through the back door of the mansion. Servants ran about calling to each other to serve tea and to make sure the dining hall was cleaned and prepped for company. At the front door, Gracelia saw her father dressed in silver armor surrounded by the men of the first squadron, on his hip was a steel broadsword the hilt wrapped in black tanned leather, dangling from the hilt was small green and white beads that shined in the light from the open door. "Papa!" Hugh turned at her voice, his face brightened at the sight of her. Kneeling down, he opened his arms for her as she flung herself into her father's arms. "Papa! You're back!" Gracelia wrapped her arms around her father's broad shoulders, the silver armor cold against her hot skin.

"Yes my little snowflake, I have returned." Hugh whispered as his arms wrapped around her tiny waist, the silk shirt smooth against his calloused palms. He closed his eyes and breathed in the familiar scent of his daughter. Her loose hairs tickling his nose as he breathed in, he wanted to stay in that moment but Gracelia's voice broke him from his thoughts.

"It's been five months! You said you'd return in four!" She huffed, poking the back of his neck. Hugh pulled away from her with a laugh, he stopped when he saw the sweat on her brow.

"You've been training, my little one." Gracelia looked down at herself, still wearing the training garb. She pulled on the shirt to get it free of the sweat on her back. He put a hand on the top of her head. "I'm sorry for taking so long, it seems the relief effort took longer than expected. Some locals weren't thrilled to see us, many of them despise the Emperor." Gracelia gasped at his words.

"Why? He's so nice and his wife is so sweet to!" Hugh smiled but it did not reach his eyes.

"Some don't think that my dear. Some still blame him for the blood war." He watched in amazement as her eyes grew into dark oceanic pools of emotion.

"But it's not even his fault! If the south had listened to him, there would have been no need for war! All he wanted was for the south and central kingdoms to come together under his rule so we could all prosper and unite. Why is that a bad thing?" Hugh laughed at her words and stood up, his hand still on top of her head.

"You have grown in these past five months, my little snowflake. My apologies for missing your birthday. But I had a gift made for you while I was away, it's in your room." Gracelia's face lit up at the mention of a gift, her eyes turning back to the sapphire blue he had missed.

"You didn't have to papa!" The young girl told him, wrapping her arms around his heavily armored legs.

"I know I didn't have to, but I wanted to." He looked at Adelina, she was scolding a maid who had spilled water on the carpet. "Adelina." She quickly turned when she heard her name.

"Yes, my lord?" She bowed to Hugh her brown hair falling over her shoulders.

"Take Gracelia up to her room and have her dress in the gift I had made for her." He winked at Adelina, she smiled at him.

"Yes, My lord! Come now young mistress." Adelina pulled Gracelia off her father's leg and led her up the stairs. "Let's go see the gift shall we?"

~~~~~~~~~

Gracelia smiled as she entered her room with Adelina, her room had changed over the course of the year. Where there was once stuffed animals now had a weapons rack and next to it was a small table adorned with steel and iron daggers in various sizes. In front of her bed was a wooden chest with the engraving of the Da Mornica sigil on the lock. "That's new! That wasn't here this morning!" Gracelia stated, astonished at the craftsmanship of the piece.

"Yes, inside is what's most important young miss." Adelina said, walking over to the chest and producing a small silver key from the folds of her dress. She inserted the key and turned it, the chest unlocked with a loud click. She gently placed her hands on the chest and pushed it open, Gracelia watched in amazement as the hinges gave a tiny protest at being used. Adelina kneeled and rummaged in the chest, once satisfied that she found the right pieces, she pulled out a small gray shirt like dress and held it up. It had the top of a dress but it wasn't long enough to touch her knees, it had a slit up the side to where her hip would be. She gently placed it on the bed and pulled out black leather pants that had ties at the ankles. "Your father had this made for you, so you can still look like a lady but be able to move freely without a pesky skirt getting in the way."

"It's beautiful!" Gracelia gently touched the fabric of the shirt like dress, much to her surprise it was soft and thick. "What is it made of?" She asked her nanny, curious.

"It's made from cotton we export from the southern region, and these pants are tanned leather. He also told the tailor to adorn the short dress with small beads shaped like snowflakes and I also told him to make the shirt any color other than light blue or white." Gracelia smiled at the thought of how much work her father must have put into deciding on what to give her for her birthday. "Do you like it?" Her nanny asked her, brushing a stray hair from the young girl's shoulder.

"I love it!" She clenched the shirt to her chest and smiled.

CHAPTER FOURTEEN

The mansion was alive with laughter and the clinking of cups in joy over the finished mission. Gracelia fidgeted outside of the dinning hall door, her little hands clasping the bottom of the dress shirt. "Are you alright, Lady Gracelia?" She turned toward the voice and blushed, feeling strange in the new clothes her father had given her. Marquis smiled as he kneeled in front of her and put a hand on her shoulder. "You look amazing, my lady. Don't worry, I'm sure your father will be happy at your attire. So smile ok?" He told the young girl in front of him, still smiling.

"OK! Thank you Marquis!" Gracelia smiled up at the man in front of her, her eyes shining. Marquis quickly looked away from the young girl, his face becoming hot. Gracelia tilted her head to look at the knight in front of her. She placed a hand on his arm. "Are you alright, Marquis?" Marquis nodded his head and quickly stood, the young girl's hand falling from his arm.

"Why don't you go in now, the lord must want to see you." He quickly stepped around her placing a hand on the wooden door in front of him. He took one last look at Gracelia in her new clothes. The shirt she was wearing met the middle of her thighs, they strapped the dagger her father had given her onto her right thigh. The slit of the shirt parting where the dagger was and her pants half hidden behind the knee high lace up leather boots. He nodded towards her before disappearing into the room, the door closing with a soft click. Gracelia ran her hands along her shirt to smooth the material. She took a step towards the door, her steps muffled on the padded carpet. She gently placed her hand against the door and pushed it open, the laughter became quiet as she entered. She looked around at the first squadron knights, all their eyes were on her. She blushed and pulled some of her hair over she shoulder, she gently ran her hands through her snow-white locks.

"My beautiful snowflake!" Hugh yelled, sauntering over to her with jagged steps. Gracelia cringed as Hugh breathed on her face, the foul scent of alcohol washing over her. "Welcome to the party! Everyone! Hasn't she grown more beautiful over the past year?" He asked the men around the table, he gently put his hand on her shoulder. After a minute of silence all the men raised their cups to the ceiling.

"Yes, my lord! A picture of beauty!" They all yelled joyously to Hugh and Gracelia. "Long live the lord and his young daughter!" Hugh laughed.

"I can drink to that!" He patted his daughter's shoulder and quickly turned away from her, staggering towards his seat. He sat down and raised his cup. "To a successful mission!" The men cheered with him, Gracelia looked at the men seated at the table, astonished. "Gracelia! Come over here! Sit beside your father!" Hugh waved to her, she walked towards him with slow and steady strides.

"Papa?" She asked once she was sitting beside him.

"Yes, my little snowflake?" He cooed at her, his breath stinging her nose. She shivered at the smell disgusted.

"I love the new clothes you got me." She smiled up at him, his eyes dark from the alcohol. He threw his head back and laughed.

"Oh, my sweet girl! I'm glad you do!" He raised his cup to his mouth.

"But there's also another thing Papa. What is the age I can marry?" Hugh spit out the alcohol in his mouth and coughed.

"I'm sorry?" He asked his daughter, wiping his mouth with his hand. Gracelia fidgeted under her father's gaze and caught Marquis looking at them in confusion. She quickly turned her eyes towards her hands, picking at her nails.

"Mama once said when I grow up I have to marry to bring honor to the family." Hugh's eyes darkened to the color of oiled water at the mention of his wife.

"This is not the place to speak of that Gracelia. I'm sorry but we will speak of your mother at the convening in two days." Gracelia gasped and looked up at her father.

"Two days? That soon?" Hugh nodded, suddenly feeling sober.

"Yes, in two days' time you will see your mother again. If you wish to not go then..."

"NO! I want to go!" Hugh looked at Gracelia in

surprise. "I want to see mother again, to show her how much I've grown in the past year papa." Gracelia looked at her father, determination filling her eyes. He nodded his head and placed his hand on the top of her head.

"All right, in two days we will head to the palace."

~~~~~~~

Two days later…

Gracelia ran towards the Empress and wrapped her arms around the woman's neck with a smile. "Auntie!" She yelled joyfully. Mazelina smiled and hugged the child to her chest.

"Hello little one!" She kissed the young girl's cheek and nuzzled her ear.

"Auntie! That tickles!" Gracelia told Mazelina while laughing. Hugh watched the two in surprise.

"A... Auntie?" Hugh asked in confusion. Gracelia looked over at her father, she was wearing a knee-length purple dress with a white ribbon tied around her waist.

"She told me to call her auntie that night a year ago when I was in her room papa. She told me to think of her like a family member because the Emperor is your war friend." Aland laughed and clasped Hugh's shoulder with his hand.

"That is correct my friend. What the young lady said is why I've been trying to get her to call me uncle." He glared at Gracelia who stuck her tongue out at him.

"Never!" She yelled teasingly with a smile. Mazelina giggled, the child still on her lap.

"Oh, come on! That's not fair! Mazie is my wife, who is your aunt! So that makes me your uncle!" Aland yelled with a smile while pointing at Gracelia.

"Auntie! He's being mean!" Gracelia yelled pointing at Aland and burying her face in Mazelina's chest.

"Oh?" Mazelina looked at her husband with a crooked smile. "Are you really being mean to little Gracie, my dear?" Aland shivered at her words and put his hands up in front of him to protect himself from what was coming.

"I... I..." Aland shook his head in defeat. Mazelina glared at her husband and stood, placing Gracelia gently on the ground.

"My dear, do you wish to seek the company of your concubines for the night?" Aland cringed at the thought of the girls in the imperial harem who the other kings had sent to him.

"N...no my dear!" The dark look in Mazelina's eyes suddenly brightened.

"Good, now!" She clapped her hands. "Time for tea!" She grabbed Gracelia's hand and pulled her towards the door to the royal parlor.

"My love, Hugh and I have business to attend to with the convening. We'll join you later, enjoy the tea." Aland said, turning his back to his wife and headed towards a different door.

"We'll be back soon Gracelia. Be a good girl,

alright?" Hugh called to his daughter, the young girl turned and pulled away from the Empress. She ran towards her father and wrapped her arms around his leg.

"I love you papa!" Gracelia yelled up at her father, Hugh smiled and kneeled down. He kissed the top of her head, spun her around and pushed her towards Mazelina.

"Go on, my little snowflake. I'll see you at dinner." He stood and turned his back to his daughter.

"Papa... If you see mama tell her I love her." Hugh froze in his tracks at her words, he turned but she had already disappeared behind the parlor door. He clenched his fist to his heart in pain.

"Gracelia... how could you ask me that..." He whispered towards the parlor door where his daughter was. He sighed and turned towards the door leaving the royal throne room behind.

CHAPTER FIFTEEN

"So how have you been over this past year Grace?" Mazelina asked the young girl in front of her, taking a sip of yellow tea. Gracelia fidgeted in her seat, her toes coming together. Mazelina's eyes tracked the movement of her feet.

"Well, I trained with the teacher you sent to my home auntie." Gracelia said, leaning forward to grab her cup.

"With that knight that the chancellor sent am I correct?" Gracelia stopped, her hands shaking. She slowly straightened herself, placing her hands on her lap as she bit her lip. "The royal trainer sent me letters on your progress. So yes, I know about that Marquis fellow and how he's been looking after you with your nanny, Adelina, while your father was away on his mission that my husband had asked him to help the citizens of our kingdom." Mazelina placed her cup down and put her elbow on the back of the couch resting her head on her hand as she watched the young girl in front of her. "Tell me about him." Gracelia looked up at Mazelina in surprise, her white hair falling over her shoulders.

"You... You really want to know about Marquis?" Her small voice shook as she said his name, her small heart thudding in her chest in rabid beats. Mazelina smiled as Gracelia's face became red.

"You have a crush on him, don't you?" Gracelia looked down at her hands, tightening her fingers into the folds of her dress. "It's all right Grace. You can tell me."

"Well... He's kind hearted and when he smiles I feel something. I don't understand this feeling," Gracelia shook her head. "I still don't understand the concept of love or marriage. Why would someone want to marry a single person knowing they could die before them?" Mazelina gasped in shock at her words. "I don't know what love is, papa tries to show me I think. I know he truly loves me but... but..." Her voice shook as her body trembled.

"What's wrong Gracie?" Mazelina asked her, eyes filling with worry.

"I don't think my mama loves me anymore Auntie." Mazelina quickly stood and walked around the table between them. She sat down and put her arms around the young girl as her eyes filled with tears.

"You don't know that my sweet girl." Mazelina told Gracelia, her hand rubbing her hair to sooth her like her mother used to. "I have something to tell you Grace." Gracelia looked up at Mazelina, her cheeks wet from falling tears. "Would you like to know?"

"Yes please auntie." Gracelia said, putting her head on the woman's chest.

"Well, a long time ago when I was your age I lived in the southern kingdom. You see that was my home, the place I was born. The sun always shined, and the sand was red, it's quite a beautiful place. However, underneath its beauty laid hatred and well my father was a cruel man, my brothers and sisters weren't any better. Since I was the youngest born from the lowest concubine, my siblings often mocked me. The maids and even my nanny told me I was a beauty that the world had never seen with my fire red hair and my black eyes. I would often come back to my mother with bruises from being bullied by my siblings. My father didn't even recognize me as his daughter at first till I got older. On my nineteenth birthday that's when the blood war began. It went one for a year before we lost, Aland had come with the Emperor prior and demanded a wife for his son at twenty-five. Hugh was with them, but he didn't say much in his black paladin armor. I was frightened at first seeing as I was afraid that we would have been in terrible danger. My father offered him my oldest sister, Bria, she was twenty-two. You see before the Emperor prior could say anything Aland had told him no and pointed, I still remember the look on my father's face. I had been hiding behind a pillar in the throne room, I was a curious girl then," Mazelina said with a giggle, continuing to rub Gracelia's hair. "My father's look of shock was funny in a way but also terrifying. Aland had walked over and yanked me from behind the pillar to stand next to him. Once his father saw how his son had looked at me that was the end of it all, they sent me off to marry Aland but what I'm trying to say is even though I didn't have the love of my father and siblings just having my mother was enough. You don't need two parents in your life my child, your father truly loves you and that should be enough." Mazelina looked down at Gracelia, the young girl was staring up at her as if hanging on her every word.

"Auntie..." She spoke in a small voice.

"Yes, my sweet girl?"

"I wish you would have been my mother instead." Mazelina gasped and smiled sadly at the girl.

"I wish too, cuss then you would have never known the hatred that comes from jealousy my girl. You're too kind for this world." Mazelina said kissing the girl's forehead. She slowly stood and looked at their tea. "We need more tea, I will return soon. I have to fetch a maid, stay here and relax." With that she left the room leaving Gracelia alone with the story of the Empress' life still running through her mind.

~~~~~~~~

Christopher listened to everything that was being said from outside the door, his ear gently pressed to the cold wood under his flushed face. "She's my mother, not yours." He whispered in anger. When he heard his mother leave he gently opened the door, stepping into the royal parlor the carpet muffling his footsteps.

"Auntie?" Called a soft voice to him as he closed the door. He quickly trekked into Gracelia's view and he heard a small gasp escape from her lips. "Crowned prince!" The young girl said, quickly standing and curtsied to him. "May the sun always shine on you, your Highness." Grinding his teeth he walked over and placed his hands on her shoulders before roughly pushing her back. He smiled at the shocked look on her face as she looked up at him from the floor.

"She's my mother! Not yours! It's not her fault that your mother is a horrid and vile woman!" He yelled at Gracelia, bending to put his face near hers. "Stay away from my mother!" He roughly pushed her shoulders again with more force than before, causing her to fall on her back. That's when they heard a scream from the other door. Christopher straightened in surprise and saw his mother with her hand over her mouth.

"CHRISTOPHER!" She yelled.

"M... Mother?" His voice shook as she sauntered towards them, her face red with anger.

"What did you do?" She asked him, kneeling beside Gracelia. Her arms quickly went around the young girl. "Well? Answer me!" She yelled at her son, her red hair flying around her face.

"I... I... I didn't..." He spoke but went quiet as Mazelina's hand struck his cheek.

"I thought I raised you better than that! She is younger than you, you are the crowned prince!" Christopher looked up at his mother in shock, his hand covering his reddened cheek. She was pointing at him, her black eyes showing no other emotion besides anger. "You will act as a crowned prince! You will never and I MEAN NEVER raise a hand against a lady as long as I live. Do you understand me, Christopher Marksman?" Mazelina asked, her face matching the color of her hair. She glared down at the young boy in front of her, ashamed and embarrassed by his actions towards Gracelia. "As the Empress of this kingdom I am the mother to all the children who have been and will be born." Christopher turned and ran away from his mother, heading towards the door he had come through. "Christopher! Wait till I tell your father!" Mazelina called after him as the door slammed shut.

"A... auntie..." Gracelia's voice shook. Mazelina quickly turned and knelt in front of the small girl.

"I'm sorry Grace. I'm so sorry my sweet girl." She cooed as she pulled the young girl into her arms, Gracelia's head resting on Mazelina's chest. "You poor thing! Your shaking!" Mazelina's arms tightened around the young girl as her small body shook from the shock of what the crowned prince had done. "Please forgive me for not being here sooner, I'm sorry for leaving you alone."

Gracelia shook her head and tightened her grip on the woman's dress, Mazelina cast a worried glance towards the door her son had disappeared through.

~~~~~~~~~

"Your majesty! You can't be serious! She is my wife's sister!" A man with black hair and even darker eyes yelled at Aland. Hugh sat beside the emperor, his head resting on the back of his hands.

"Hugh is also Juliana's husband Or did you forget that Maverick? Seeing as he is your brother-in-law." Aland said to the black-haired man named

102

Maverick. They were sitting in the council room, all the nobles had gathered for Juliana's trial.

"My lord, but banishing her to the northern temple would surely be a disgrace against the Goddess herself seeing as she blessed Duke Da Mornica's daughter." An elderly man spoke, his fingers twirling his white beard. Beside him his eldest son sat in silence, just listening to the men before him.

"Lord Octavick, I am the high priestess of the northern temple," Stated a young woman with silver hair, she had beads in all shapes and colors in her hair. Her gold-colored eyes shone like stars. "I held a meeting of my own in the temple to discuss this matter with my fellow priestess and priests. We all agreed that she should be sent to the temple that the Goddess lives in to confess her sins and hopefully be able to enter the Goddess' garden when her earthly shell dies." Hugh sighed as the others yelled over each other.

"That would be a disgrace against the Goddess!"

"She doesn't deserve it!"

"I say we kill her and be done with it!"

"Have you gone mad? That'll kill her young daughter and possibly even scar her!"

"ENOUGH!" Aland yelled, slamming his hand down onto the table. When it was quiet he continued. "Why don't we let Hugh speak on his daughter's behalf seeing as she is not here at the moment." Aland pointed to Hugh, who hadn't spoken during the argument. Hugh slowly stood from his seat and placed his hands on the table, looking at the men before him.

"I agree with Priestess Lilia on the matter. If the Goddess has agreed to have her banished to the temple to live out the rest of her years there, then so be it. I will not have the mother of my child beheaded or killed before my child's eyes! I will not allow such darkness to taint her precious soul!" He yelled, his eyes flashing to every member of the council before him. "She is more precious than life itself! I would gladly go to war for her, just to see her smile! She is my one and only child! If I die before I see her grow up the one man I would want looking after my daughter is him!" Hugh pointed towards Marquis who was standing beside the door in silence wearing a purple jacket with silver trimmings. He looked up in surprise at what Hugh had just said.

"My lord! What are you saying?" He asked in confusion.

"I've seen the way my daughter looks and acts around you! If anyone were to take my place I'd rather it be you, Marquis." Hugh stated without a change in emotion, he turned his attention back at the men in attendance. Ignoring the objection that was surely coming from Marquis' mouth. "If that does not prove how much I care for my daughter then you're all foolish and filled with God like arrogance! Maverick," He looked at the dark-haired man. "Surely your wife told you about all the horrid things that Juliana did to her when she was a child?

Pulling her hair and threatening to hit her if she didn't do what Juliana told her to do?" Maverick opened his mouth to object before closing it again, ashamed. "That's what I thought," He turned his attention back to the other men. "All of you! What if she was your daughter? What if Gracelia was your child? Would you want to kill her mother right in front of her? Or banish her to the northern kingdom, you decide what you would want if you were in my shoes." He quickly turned away from the table and headed towards the door. Aland smiled at his friend's back, seeing the old Hugh from the days of the blood war.

"My lord..." Marquis stated.

"Not now!" Hugh yelled at him pulling the door open. Marquis quickly followed him, shutting the door behind them. They all stared dumbfounded at the door, neither one saying a word as Aland's laugh rang throughout the room.

CHAPTER SIXTEEN

The other nobles crowded the throne room when Gracelia entered the room, hand in hand with her father, Marquis following close behind. "Duke Da Mornica! The Emperor has reserved a spot for you and your daughter at the front, nearest the thrones." A royal guard told them pushing people aside as he escorted the three through the crowd of nobles.

"What's a child doing here?"

"That's strange, children can't see the trial."

"Shut up, you idiots! That's Gracelia Da Mornica, the child blessed by the Goddess."

Everyone gasped and watched as the young girl passed by them. "Papa?" Gracelia asked when they were standing below the throne.

"Yes, my little snowflake?" Hugh looked down at his daughter, her hair braided over her shoulder with flower pins adorning the interact twist. She was wearing a floor length black dress with a blue sash tied around her waist.

"Will mama recognize me?" Before Hugh could answer, Marcus announced the Emperor and Empress.

"May the sun always shine on you, your majesties." The crowd all said as one, bowing and curtsying to the royals before them.

"Thank you, my loyal citizens. You all know we are to lay punishment to a woman who has been found guilty of greed and malicious intent towards her own blood." Aland sat on his throne, his crown on his head. Mazelina sat after her husband, her hair pulled back into a bun on top of her head with her circlet resting on her forehead. "Enter!" Aland yelled towards the door they had all walked through moments before. The door opened with a loud creak and in the doorway stood a woman.

Her brown hair covered her face, her dress covered in dirt and her shackled wrists in front of her. The guards pushed her forward and the chains rattled against the cold tile floor as she moved. Gracelia felt a hand rest on her shoulder, she looked up to see Marquis looking down at her, worry filling his eyes. She patted his hand with hers and watched as her mother came to a stop in front of the dais.

"Juliana."

"Your highnesses." Juliana told them in a frail voice, her body was thin and her hair matted from sleeping in the dungeon below the castle.

"It has been a year." Aland said, waiting to see how she would react.

"Yes, your grace. It has been a year." Mazelina smiled at the frail woman in front of her, satisfied with the way things were going between Juliana and Aland.

"You are here to receive your punishment for the crimes you committed. What do you have to say against this matter?" Juliana slowly raised her head, her hair falling around her face. Her dark brown eyes burning with hatred towards the two in front of her. Mazelina bit the inside of her cheek, Aland stared down at her knowing she wouldn't challenge him.

"I will take whatever punishment you have, my lord." Juliana told the two royals in front of her, hate filled her heart as she saw Mazelina looking down at her with anger. Before Aland could speak a voice rang out in the silent room, a voice filled with love.

"MAMA!" Gracelia ran towards her mother, Marquis' hand outstretched towards her to yank the child back to her father's side. Gracelia wrapped her arms around the thin woman, smiling from ear to ear. "Hi mama!" Juliana went rigged at the sound of her child's voice, her cheek resting on Juliana's cheek. "I've missed you." Juliana lifted her hands and roughly pushed Gracelia away from her the chains rattling against each other. The young girl looked at her mother in shock as she fell to the ground.

"You are not my child! You are not my Gracelia! You are a monster! You're a changeling! Bring me my sweet girl back!" Gracelia stood, her face hidden in shadow as she slowly took a step towards her mother. Juliana tried to get away from the girl but before she could Gracelia was on top of her. The obsidian blade held to Juliana's throat, Gracelia stared into her mother's brown eyes with her storm gray ones.

"I am me, mother. I am not a changeling, I am Gracelia and will always be Gracelia. You are mad, you've lost your mind. I should kill you for all the things you've done..." Gracelia told Juliana, moving

the blade closer to the woman's neck when suddenly
a pair of arms went around her waist. "Let me go!"
She screamed as the blade fell from her hand onto
the cold floor.

"Enough!" Marquis yelled as Gracelia struggled
in his grasp.

"Marquis! Put me down! She deserves to die!"
Gracelia struggled harder, kicking at him and
scratching his arms with her nails. Everyone
watched in horror as the young girl's eyes had
grown dark, as dark as the ocean during a storm.
Juliana looked at the blade next to her and went to
grab it when a strong hand went around the hilt of
the blade.

"Juliana."

"Hugh..." Juliana looked up at her husband who
had betrayed her, his hands quickly covering the
dagger with a cloth before slipping it into the pocket
of his suit jacket. He had dark circles under his
eyes, his once bright eyes that showed her love were
now dull as he looked at her with nothing but
contempt. "Why...?" She asked him, her hands
shaking.

"You did it to yourself. I will raise our daughter
alone without you." Juliana looked up at Hugh in
shock.

"She needs a mother..." Juliana said, reaching
towards Hugh with her shackled hands. Before she
could touch him, a fan smacked her hands away.
Juliana looked up to see Mazelina holding the fan to
her face. The Empress looked at the frail defeated

woman in front of her, her black eyes void of emotion.

"She has a mother, two mothers in fact. Adelina and I, the Empress of this kingdom." Juliana gasped at the Empress, the fire of hatred dying in her eyes to give way to sadness.

"Your grace, you have your own child! Don't steal mine!" Juliana wailed at Mazelina, tears streaming down her dirty face creating rivers on her cheeks. Mazelina chuckled at the woman, she looked over at Gracelia who had now calmed but was still staring at Juliana with malice and hatred.

"Enough with the chatter. My dear husband, give her the punishment." Mazelina said to Aland as she climbed the steps back to her seat. She watched as Marquis carried the young girl back to where they had stood before. Gracelia looked up at the knight in annoyance at being stopped, Hugh spoke softly to Marquis, he nodded. Marquis turned towards the nearest door with Gracelia still in his arms.

~~~~~~~~~

Once the door had shut behind the two, Aland looked down at the woman below him. "Juliana, Your punishment is to reside in the northern kingdom where you will live out the rest of your years in the Goddess of Winter's temple. High priestess Lilia was the one to bring up the idea. The council agreed to it and now you will stay in the frigid north. Guards!" Juliana looked up at Aland in shock and dismay.

"Your highness! Please!" Juliana yelled,

struggling against the hands that held her. Lilia stepped away from where she had been hiding and walked up to the blessed snow's mother, she placed her hand gently on the woman's forehead.

"Sleep." Lilia said, when she removed her hand Juliana was fast asleep in the guard's hands. She turned and curtsied to Aland and Mazelina. "She will remain asleep until our arrival at the temple in two days' time. Goddess bless you, your highnesses and may the sun always shine on you." She straightened and turned to leave the room, following the guards.

"Safe travels Priestess." The Nobles all said as they nodded their heads at her, Lilia nodded back as her elf ears poked from underneath her silver hair. Everyone watched in fascination at seeing a real northern elf for the first time, Lilia moved her hair to hide her ears and quickly shut the door behind her leaving the eyes that followed her behind.

~~~~~~~~

Two weeks later...

Hugh sat at his desk, the hard wood top covered in reports, glimpsing white hair in the sunlight outside his window. He watched his daughter spar with her own personal knight Marquis, after the incident at the convening Marquis had given Gracelia a knight's oath. Hugh rubbed his face with his hands and yawned. When there was a knock on the door. "Come in." The door opened and Sir Lee, his second in command, walked in holding a silver envelope. "What is it?" Hugh asked as Lee put the envelope on the desk.

"It's from the Temple of Winter, my lord." Hugh's eyes grew wide as he looked at the letter in front of him, laying among the reports that Aland had sent him to fix. With shaking hands Hugh reached towards the envelope, softly grabbing it with two fingers. He slowly broke the wax seal and opened it, inside was a letter. He pulled the letter from the envelope and opened it. "What does it say my lord?" Lee asked Hugh, curious. Hugh licked his lips and began.

"To Duke Da Mornica, I regret to inform you of Juliana's death. Two days ago a priest and I found her hanging in her room from the rafters with the bed sheet tied around her neck. A chair was below her seeming she had kicked it, my deepest apologies to you and your young daughter. May the Goddess heal your hurt and your heart. Best regards, High Priestess Lilia."

Hugh sighed as his heart tightened in his chest, feeling like a snake coiling around it. Lee looked at Hugh with Pity.

"I'm sorry, my lord." Hugh shook his head and covered his face with his hands as tears spilled from his eyes.

"It's not me you should say sorry to... it's my daughter who should worry you..." Hugh uncovered his face and looked out the window at his young daughter, smiling and laughing with the other men. "What am I going to tell her is the question..."

ABOUT THE AUTHOR

My name is Sierra Conrady and I love to write all kinds of different genres. This book has taken me over a year to make and it is only book one of a three part series titles <u>The Noble Huntress</u>. I am a 22 year old who lives in Birdsboro, Pennsylvania but I was originally born in San Antonio, Texas and moved from place to place because my family was military. I have pet rats that I adore and they make me happy. I've been writing stories since I was a kid, the first book that gave me that creative spark was Disney's The Little Mermaid. Thanks to that story, I was finally able to see what I wanted to be. To those reading this, never give up on your dreams because they will come true.

Sneak Peak
Light and Shadow

Ten Years Later…

The sunlight shined through the curtains hitting
the woman's closed eyes; she groaned as she pulled
the blue comforter with lotus flower stitchings over
her face. She sat up once she knew that sleep would
evade her; she stretched her arms over her head and
yawned. The young woman looked at her curtains
as the sun hit her eyes. "Good morning." She told
the sun, she threw off her covers and put her feet on
the plush carpet. She smiled as she wiggled her
toes, feeling the softness of the carpet against her
feet. She stood up and walked over to her vanity,
scratching the top of her head as she went. She
stopped and looked at her reflection.

Her sapphire blue eyes still as bright as they were
when she was a kid, her snow white hair had grown
longer and now rested at the middle of her back.
She grabbed her brush and yanked the bristles
through her curls, cringing as it connected with the
knots in her hair. She sighed as the brush went
through her hair softly, happy that she finally could
tame her hair without Adelina's help. She sighed
sadly from the realization she was on her own.

Adelina had gotten married to the tailor that had
made all of her clothes and still did. He was the
only man in town that Adelina admired more than
her brother and deceased father. The young women
smiled at the memory of Adelina in her dress that
the tailor had made for her, the way the sleeves had
billowed around her wrists made the woman sigh in

jealousy. She shook her head and whispered to herself. "You're eighteen now and you could marry if you understood the concept of it that is." She stood up and went to her door, still in her nightgown, she opened the door slightly and saw Marquis through the crack. She admired how he'd only gotten more handsome. She felt her face growing hot as she looked at him in admiration. His once short black hair had grown to cover the top of his ears, he always cut it to keep it short but she liked the way it looked long. She gasped when Marquis caught her looking at him, he smiled and bowed his head.

"Good Morning Lady Gracelia." She looked away from him, hiding her face behind the door.

"G... Good morning Marquis." She told him in a soft tone she only used for him.

"Good morning my Lady!" Gracelia looked back and saw Alexander standing in front of Marquis with a giant smile on his face. He had grown his hair out as he aged, what was once cropped and well kept was now shaggy and long.

"Good Morning to you too Alexander." She told him in a monotone type voice. The knight put his hand on the door and made a pouting face. Even though he was older than her, he still acted like a child.

"My lady that's not fair! You're always mean," He looked at Marquis for help. "Marquis help me!" Marquis laughed as he put his hand on the young knight's shoulder.

"Leave it be Alex." He told Alexander with a smile. "Get back to your position."

"But..." Marquis looked at him with annoyance.

"What did I say?" Alexander looked at Marquis like he'd just gotten slapped.

"Yes, sir." Gracelia watched in amazement at the confrontation that had just occurred in front of her. Marquis watched Alexander step away from the door and back to his position, he looked at Gracelia.

"Please get dressed my lady. It's time for breakfast." Marquis told her as he put his hand on the doorknob and closed it, shutting her in her room. Gracelia looked at the door in annoyance and huffed at it.

"I'm not a kid anymore Marquis." She whispered as she turned around and walked to her wardrobe. She put her hand on the thick wood and smiled as she remembered her fifteenth birthday. Her father had the wardrobe made for her and carved with snowflakes falling on a lotus pond. She'd fallen in love with the Empress' royal garden that had a lotus pond in it when she had visited the royal family during the new year's ball during that year.

She pulled it open and ran her finger across all the gowns, loving the texture of the: silk, cotton and velvet fabrics against her skin. She stopped at a dark blue dress and pulled it out, she placed it on her bed and examined it. The dress had ivy vines stitched into the skirt and stopped at the waist of the dress. She smiled at the craftsmen ship of Adelina's husband.

Printed in Great Britain
by Amazon